Sa'id Salaam Presents

# Salty Chicks
# &
# Sweet Licks:
# Sex, Money, Murder 2
A Novel By
**Sa'id Salaam**

# Chapter 1

"Hmp," Sharon grunted at her reflection. Her matching undergarments perfectly framed her firm frame. She carefully slid a dress overhead so she wouldn't muss her curls. She decided hose looked too old fashion and went with her lovely shaved legs instead. She felt beautiful and that should have been enough but still stepped into the living room for a second opinion.

"Un uh! What you all dressed up for?" Reign fussed as she hopped to her feet.

"I told you I'm going out with Miss Simone tonight," she replied. "How I look?"

"You cool," she replied since she didn't know how to give a proper compliment. She saw the dejected look on her mother's face and tried again. "I mean, you look dope! Don't bring me no step pops tonight!"

"You really think guys would...like me?" she asked hopefully. Guys did, and flirted all the time. Sharon just had tunnel vision about taking care of her family and missed most of it.

"Ma, you hot! Dudes gone be all over you!" she assured. "I'm surprised you really going out!"

"Well, yeah. After Reef, you getting pregnant, and now my job..." Sharon sighed.

"What about your job, ma?" Reign moaned.

Sharon realized she hadn't the bad news or good news that followed. "Nothing, I just took a better position at Harlem Hospital," she said, combining the two and liking how it sounded.

A knock on the door cut the conversation short when Reign rushed to open it.

"You ready? Oh, yeah you are! Oh my, you look good! Luckily I got a man cuz you gone get all the attention!" Simone gushed as she and Unique came in. Unique had her overnight bag since she was staying the night.

"You think?" Sharon blushed. It had been so long since she'd felt sexy that she didn't know just how sexy she was.

"Girl, yes! You fierce! Let's go turn up," Simone said and led the way out to the street.

They were too cute for the bus so they hailed a gypsy cab once they reached Ogden Avenue.

"Fire this up," Unique sang once they were alone as she came out with a blunt.

"Where you get weed from?" Reign asked since it was getting harder to come by. Her brother was no longer around to break her off and her mother was struggling just to keep the bills paid.

"Bryan gave me some money. He always giving me money," she stated as if she didn't understand why.

"Tuh!" Reign huffed since she knew why. "Girl, he want some of that young snatch. That's why he keep breaking you off."

"You think? Eww! I wish I would fuck behind my moms! They be getting it in too!'" she laughed.

Bryan and Simone didn't even wait until she went to sleep anymore. It was like he was trying to get all he could before she started showing. Reign, Unique and Simone were starting to round out but it couldn't be seen in clothes.

"Well, I hope my moms meet a guy. She lonely. Plus, we could use some help around here," Reign admitted.

"What about us? You think we'll ever find someone else? I don't want no one but Reef but..." Unique wondered aloud.

"I never thought about it. I'm pregnant by a dude I would never be with, even if he wasn't going to jail," she replied.

They both sank deep in thought as the blunt went back and forth.

*****

"This is it! It look like it's lit!" Simone cheered when they reached the Manhattan hotspot.

Sharon smiled at her sounding like her daughter but also because she was actually going into a club. "Wow!" Sharon exclaimed then second guessed herself seeing the sexy twenty-somethings in line. She blushed at one child with a neckline that plunged to her navel, exposing half her chest. Little did she know, Reign had the same blouse in a knockoff version.

"Nuh uh, girl! No you don't!" Simone fussed when she guessed what was on her mind. "These young broads ain't got nothing on us. They young and dumb but we grown and sexy. We career women."

"We are," Sharon agreed since running a cash register is a career. An honorable one at that. She lifted her head and fell into the line of women hoping to be selected by the eligible men inside.

The line inched forward until Sharon and Simone were granted access inside the club. Sharon let out another 'wow' as she checked out the scenery. She'd never been inside of a club before. The closest she'd even come was when she went to a bar with her ex-husband Roscoe. The dim lights and the smell of cologne and alcohol brought back vivid memories that momentarily engulfed her.

*"Yo, the dude name is Sweet. He stay posted up at the bar with a broad," Roscoe briefed when they pulled up to the Harlem bar.*

*"Well, if he with a girl, why he gonna talk to me?" 17-year-old Sharon asked in confusion.*

*Roscoe smiled at the silly question that came with training a young girl. He was only 22 at the time but the young girl from Long Island was as green as a bag of good weed. Not to mention fine as wine with a big round behind. "Cuz you a fine young thing and pimps love fine young things," he explained and planted a kiss on her thick lips.*

*Young Sharon had aspirations to be a nurse and Roscoe had promised to help her. In return, she helped him in his career of robbing numbers men, heroin dealers, and his favorite, pimps. All three kept pockets full of dead presidents but he preferred dead pimps too.*

*"Oh!" She smiled brightly at both the compliment and understanding the plan. She was bait like a worm on a hook with that natural wiggle in her walk.*

*"Just get him out to the alley and I got it from there," Roscoe explained with another kiss to her plump lips.*

*"Okay," she said and hopped out the car.*

*Roscoe almost felt sorry for Sweet as he watched her walk inside. He was definitely going to go for her, hoping to fuck, but he was the only one who was getting fucked tonight.*

*Sharon put a little extra in her walk for her man then fussed at herself for missing another opportunity to give him the news. She was pregnant but wouldn't know if the news was good or bad until she got his reaction. She figured he had to expect with it the way he stayed inside of her. He always pushed in instead of pulling out, so it was just a matter of time and that time was now.*

*"So I told that bitch I'm a mothafucking pimp not a... Dayum!" Sweet exclaimed when young Sharon walked in and interrupted his pimp tales.*

*All eyes shot over to the pretty young thing. The way her hips spread gave a hint of what she was toting behind her. One of those asses so fat it could be seen from the front.*

*"Damn, she fine!" Sweet's bottom bitch cheered. "Get her, daddy! I wanna taste that too!"*

*"Oh, I got her!" he vowed and made his approach. His fancy strut and loud colors reminded Sharon of a peacock but she couldn't laugh at the moment. "What you drinking, sugar?"*

*"Seven and 7, please," she replied. Sharon wasn't much of a drinker back then but that's what her man drank. She would have a sip whenever he lifted his glass to her lips.*

*"That's a man's drink. Can you handle a man?" he asked and licked his thick purple lips trying to be seductive.*

*"Let's step outside and see," she dared and led the way.*

*Sweet followed her out into the alley as if hypnotized by the swaying hips in front of him. He got so hard so fast that his vision got blurry. Not so blurry to not see the pistol in his face when Roscoe jumped out from behind a dumpster like a jack-in-the-box.*

*"Well I'll be damned," Sweet fussed when he realized what just happened.*

*"Yeah, you will," Roscoe laughed. He could afford to laugh since the gun in his hand was dead serious. "Go on back to the car, babe."*

*"'Kay. Hurry up, baby," she purred and walked away.*

*Sweet was already in trouble but dug his own grave by looking down the alley at Sharon's ass as she walked away.*

*"You may as well go on with her. Here you go, my man," Sweet said and handed over all the cash from one of his pockets.*

*"Appreciate it but I'ma need all yo dough, my man," Roscoe demanded. He was a street dude and knew street dudes keep money in different places for situations just like this.*

*The pimp twisted his lips and came off every dollar from every pocket and both socks. "That's it!" he snarled and squinted to memorize the face.*

*"Thanks," Roscoe said quite politely then shot him in his face rather rudely. He turned and rushed towards the car but Sharon was rushing back towards him.*

*"Are you okay? Heard a shot!" she said, looking him over for bullet holes.*

*"I'm good. We gotta go," he urged. "Come on, Sharon. Sharon..."*

"Um, Sharon?" Simone laughed as she snatched the woman back into the present.

"This is nice!" she cheered as she looked around the quaint bar. All eyes were on her since she was a new face. Most of the regular dudes had already run through most of the regular girls who frequented the place. For the next few hours, various men introduced themselves and fed them drinks. By the end of the night Sharon had a purse full of numbers but not one caught her attention enough to want to call.

The women split a taxi ride back uptown.

"I had fun!" Sharon admitted when they got out on 164th Street.

"Girl, me too! We gotta do this again!" Simone declared. She'd gotten a couple of numbers to just in case things didn't work out with Bryan.

"Sure! Not sure when I can get off again but, sure," she agreed and went upstairs. She peeked in on the girls sleeping together in the same bed. They almost looked like the little angels they once were except the remnants of weed smoke lingering in the air and them both being pregnant. She let out a sigh and eased back out the room and entered her own.

"Whew!" she cheered when she stepped down out of her heels. It had been so long since she'd worn a pair that she forgotten just how uncomfortable they could be. She was quite tipsy, if not drunk, so putting clothes in the hamper could wait. It would have to wait because she let her clothes fall to the floor as she stripped out of them. One of Reef's t-shirts had become her favorite nightgowns so she slid into one and under her covers.

"Mmmm," Sharon moaned when her hand found her neglected vagina under her sheets. It was fat and hairy from being virtually ignored for almost a decade. She forgot how wet and slippery it could get until it got all wet and slippery on her fingers. So wet and slippery that a finger easily slipped inside. It was a tight fit but she still worked it in and out. A minute later, her legs kicked and bucked as she busted the first nut of the night. It was the first but would not be the last and she went for seconds the second the first one subsided.

"What the heck was that?" Unique asked when they heard a roar from across the hall. They had only pretended to be asleep when they heard Sharon come in so they were still awake when she came.

"Ooh, I think my moms getting laid!" Reign exclaimed and covered her mouth. She uncovered it and announced, "Good for her."

*****

"Guess I gotta cook my own breakfast," Reign grumbled like the spoiled child she was. She and Unique rolled out of bed just before noon and Sharon was still in bed.

"We can do it!" Unique said hopefully. Both girls could fight, shoot, roll blunts and bag weed but neither could scramble an egg if their lives depended on it.

"Yeah, we can! Shoot, we gonna be mothers soon, too! We can cook some damn breakfast!" she shot back.

"I want some eggs, bacon and...um, hash browns! Yeah, hash browns," Unique said and nodded.

Reign nodded too and they set out to make breakfast. It was about as successful as their first lick and soon black smoke filled the room.

"What the hell is going on out here? Reign! What's burning?" Sharon shrieked when she rushed out to respond to the blaring fire alarms.

"I was tryna make eggs," Reign whined and pointed to the blackened eggs in the pan.

"Well, did you put butter in the pan? And the flame is way too high!" Sharon fussed and put out the fire. She let out a frustrated sigh and regained her composure. "Let me teach you two how to cook. You can't feed them babies hot chips and quarter water!"

Reign and Unique smiled and paid close attention to their first cooking lesson. They snickered and giggled like conspirators until Sharon realized it was about her.

"What?" she challenged and twisted her lips.

"We heard you last night!" Unique laughed and ducked.

"Mmhm, so bring him out! Let's see him!" Reign demanded.

Her mother turned beet red from embarrassment. "No, I..." she started then stopped since the truth was more embarrassing than their assumption. "There is no one in my room. You can check."

Reign took the bait and rushed down the hall. She entered her mother's room and looked around, under and in but came up empty. "He gone!" she told Unique and twisted her lips.

"Ooh, my moms used to try to sneak dudes out early in the morning, too!" Unique recalled. It was just as futile since she could hear the sex from the next room.

"Yeah, well, breakfast is ready. Next time you girls are cooking," Sharon demanded and served the plates.

"You gone have a baby, too?" Unique asked as they ate.

"Girl, put some food in your mouth so you can't ask silly questions! I'm almost forty years old. I work twenty hours a day..." she said, rattling off excuses and reasons. She left out the main one which was not having a man.

What she wanted most was a man.

# Chapter 2

"Un uh! Say word!" Neta demanded when both Reign and Unique's baby bumps seemed to appear out of nowhere. Both had entered their second trimester and their bellies suddenly popped out.

"Word," Reign nodded and confirmed they were both pregnant.

"She copied me!" Unique added and laughed.

"And I followed you two!" Jewel added and touched her still flat stomach. "Dang, Seven ain't never wanna use no rubber."

"You pregnant by Seven?" Unique demanded so forcefully that everyone present frowned curiously. She heard it too and tried to clean it up. "I mean, so!"

"Wait, who you pregnant by, Reign?" Neta needed to know. Everyone knew by now that Kidd had killed her brother and that Tito almost killed Kidd, so it didn't even cross her mind that he'd planted the seed growing in her belly.

"Nobody y'all know," Reign said and looked to Unique for help.

"Yeah, I told her don't be messing with them Brooklyn niggas! Nigga knocked her up then got knocked off," she adlibbed.

"So, who you pregnant by?" Jewel asked and held her breath in hopes that she wouldn't say Seven. Unique started to just to spite her but the truth trumped it like an ace of spades.

"Her brother," Unique said, pointing at Reign and tilted her head in pride. All heads snapped to Reign for confirmation and got it.

"Yup. Her sneaky butt was messing with him for months," Reign said. She'd watched the video enough to know.

"Wow!" Neta said, looking at Unique in awe. She actually gave Reef some head one night but kept it to herself just like the load of semen she swallowed at the end of it.

"Dang!" Jewel added, since she too only got to swallow his babies. It was nothing to brag about in general but especially in front of the chick carrying his kid.

9

"Hmp!" Mia huffed too since she, too, had to swallow to get his babies in her belly. All three of them, plus several others, wished they were the one he'd made love to. The one with his child growing inside them.

"What y'all got going on?" Reign challenged but they quickly played it off. The change in weather prevented them from walking to the train so they talked loudly on the back of the bus.

"Nothing," the three said quickly and looked out the window. Reign had no idea some of the body parts in his phone belonged to them. The subject was changed several more times as they made their way to school.

"Look at these hoes!" Zeta laughed when she and the 170th Street Crew boarded the train. "Can't even fuck without getting knocked up."

"Yo, how you know they ain't wanna have a baby? Huh?" Neta demanded and inched forward for battle.

"A'ight yo, don't end up stretched out like your girls!" Zeta's sidekick JoJo challenged. She had moved up to second once Leticia got killed and Zeta moved up to head hoe in charge.

"Don't end up like that lab rat looking bitch either!" Jewel said, stepping up too.

"Chill, y'all. Them broke broads just hungry. Food stamps don't come til next week," Unique laughed but didn't want to fight.

"Yeah, they ain't talking 'bout nothing!" Reign added since she didn't want to fight either. She still planned to get them back for stomping her but would not risk losing her baby.

"That's what I thought!" Zeta snarled and slid a box cutter from her coat sleeve.

The tensions subsided as they separated for the rest of the ride to school. Both Unique and Reign breathed a sigh of relief and put their hands on their bellies. Bellies that grew with every passing day.

\*\*\*\*\*

"Look!" Unique warned when they reached the block and saw Rankin laughing with Tito and the rest of the dope boys. He was the connect so they laughed when he laughed. Except Seven who stopped laughing when he saw Unique first, then Jewel.

"Um?" Reign hummed. She had successfully ducked and dodged him since the rape. She made sure to check out her window for his car anytime she left her building. She got tired of ducking and dodging and changed course.

"Girl, what you doing?" Unique fussed in a hush as she marched straight towards Rankin and company.

"So mi lick a shot 'pon dem!" Rankin recalled some of his Kingston war stories. He stopped dead in his tracks when he saw Reign headed his way. His eyes went wide when he saw her round stomach leading the way. He knew he'd gone too far when he'd violated the girl in a drunken rage. He wasn't sure how these young goons would react so he mentally reached for the gun in his back in case things went south.

"Un huh, see what you did? Knock me up and now act like you don't know me!" she spat to the shock of everyone.

Who had fucked Reign and got her pregnant had been the talk of the trap since she began to show. Every one of them had tried to fuck her secretly before Reef died, then openly after his funeral. Most assumed it was Seven since he was the resident pretty boy. He was destined to be baby daddy to many.

"I, I, um?" the dread stammered in shock. He may have been drunk but he vividly remembered the blood she'd left on his dick. He assumed it was from her cherry and not the tears in her walls from the rough sex. He also recalled busting several nuts inside that good young pussy.

"'Um' nothing. You gotta do better than that!" she demanded and extended her palm. It was empty when she stuck it out but would be full when she pulled it back.

"Ya, mon," he nodded and broke bread. He dug into a pocket and produced a roll of cash. He handed it over without even counting it. Whatever it was, that good young pussy was well worth it.

"Thanks," she said and spun on her heels. Unique was so stunned she was stuck until Reign called her. "Come on, Neek!" she summoned and snapped her out of her daze.

"Girl! Yo! What you doing?" Unique pleaded when they entered Reign's building.

"I don't know," Reign admitted. "I just wasn't gonna keep running from that nigga! Now I'ma milk that bumba clot for everything I can then we gonna rob his blood clot ass!"

*****

"Sup with you, shorty?" Tito asked when he walked up behind Unique in the bodega. He gripped her booty with both hands just like he did when he sexed her. She could smell Hennessy on his breath when he tried to kiss her.

"Stooop," she whined and spun out of his grasp. "I'm pregnant."

"I know. I like pregnant pussy. Taste like plantains," he laughed and groped her again. "You sure it ain't mine? Didn't I bust in you?"

"It ain't yours!" she whined and pouted. She vividly recalled having a period between anyone else and Reef. No one touched her after Reef so there was no question in her mind.

"My man Reef was all up in there, huh?" he said and reached around to palm her ass once more. "No wonder he told niggas to leave you alone. He gone now. Come on up to my apartment and let me smash."

"No, stop," Unique whined and struggled to free herself. She looked to papi behind the counter for help and got some. The older Puerto Rican said something in rapid fire Spanish that made Tito raise his hands in surrender and back away. Unique forgot her items and ran out the store.

"Girl, what's wrong with you?" Reign fussed when she answered the urgent knock.

Unique ran in and locked the door behind her. "Dang Tito! He was pawing all over me, tryna get me to come to his house!" she said, out of breath from the sprint up the stairs.

"Why you ain't go?" Reign reeled and frowned.

"Go? Why? I'on want him!" she asked in confusion.

"Girl, how we gone get that bag if we don't get in?" she reminded.

"Yeah, but he want some pussy. He ain't getting none!" Unique said like he hadn't gotten it already.

"Nah, you ain't gotta fuck him. We just need to get inside so we can rob his ass," Reign reminded and retreated into her head to formulate a plot. A wicked grin spread on her pretty face when one came to mind.

"What?" Unique asked, seeing the devious smirk on her face.

"He keep tryna get us up to his apartment, so we need to go. He gone think he gone fuck us but we gonna fuck him. With this...." she said and reached under the cushion. Unique's eyes went wide when she came up with the silencer equipped pistol.

"Oooh!" Unique cheered and grabbed the gun. Reef had taught them both how to shoot using this one so they both knew how to use it. Both could hit a target from ten feet away. A decent distance since most gun fights are much closer. "He ain't gone let us just take his money."

"Of course not. That's why you gonna have to bust him," she said.

"Me! Why me?" Unique shrieked. "Why not you?"

"Okay," Reign shrugged and took the gun back. Tito had violated when he'd pushed them down and she didn't mind making him pay. Her brother was in a box and she didn't mind putting someone else in one.

"Bet. We need to catch him before he re-up from Rankin. We need that bread, fuck the weed," Unique surmised.

"Saturday, so we gotta get him Friday night after he collect," Reign said since Tito mimicked what her brother did. Many a Friday night she'd walked in on Reef counting stacks.

"Okay, Friday it is," she agreed.

Tito had two more days to live and didn't even know it.

*****

Sharon was back to working doubles at Harlem Hospital and was still single. None of the numbers she got from the club panned out. The first one she called, some woman answered and fussed her out about calling her man. She tried another one but some man answered and fussed her out about calling his man.

Sharon was on the verge of giving up. There were plenty doctors, male nurses, paramedics and other men in and out the hospital but she was largely overlooked. Not surprising since the other women, younger than her age and even older, dressed to impress while she remained plain as Jane. She was going to have to step her game up if she was going to get a man. She wanted one too because she was getting cramps in her hand from playing in her pussy almost daily.

"Hmp?" Sharon huffed at her reflection as she got dressed for work. She'd gone from a size 10 to a 12 and had bought some larger pants to conceal all that extra ass. "You know what?" she dared herself and went back into her closet and pulled out the smaller scrubs and squeezed into them. She turned sideways to check her booty and nodded approvingly. Her ass looked great pressing the purple fabric and showing a little panty line.

"You going to work?" Reign asked in general but frowned at her tight pants.

"You don't, so somebody has to," she snapped. Sharon knew it was uncalled for but didn't take it back. She did soften her tone before going on, "Make sure you drink plenty water. And stop smoking."

"Okay, ma," she said and rubbed her belly. She stretched out on the sofa in her night clothes and flicked the remote.

Sharon twisted her lips at her knowing that didn't mean she was in for the night. She bit her tongue because it didn't matter much anymore since she was already pregnant.

Sharon bundled up for the New York winter night and headed off for work. The commute was twice as long as her old job since she had to travel to Manhattan. She filled the void by giggling and shaking her head while reading the latest Sa'id Salaam classic. And who could blame her because that's some good shit.

"Here we go," she sighed when she arrived at work to see two ambulances pulling up at the same time. The Bronx was bad but Harlem was no better. Every night was a marathon of gunshot victims, stabbing victims, domestic victims and other assorted victims. She clocked in and jumped right into the fray.

"Multiple GSW, torso, leg and both arms!" a paramedic announced as he wheeled in a blood soaked patient on a blood soaked gurney.

Sharon looked at the patient then up to the man speaking. She cocked her head curiously, then placed the face. "Bryan? Right?" she asked.

He had been in full paramedic mode until he heard his name called. "Yeah, do I know you?" he asked and frowned when he failed to place the face. He was pretty sure he would have remembered this pretty face and the name that went with it.

"Not yet..." she said flirtatiously but wasn't sure why. She knew she was a better catch than Simone and deserved a man. They made googly eyes and small talk over the bleeding victim.

"Yo, just get her number, B!" the patient pleaded so he could get into surgery.

"That's a good idea," Sharon agreed and quickly jotted her digits.

"I'll hit you later," Bryan said and backed away to get back to work.

"I'm counting on it," she giggled at her naughty entendre. She felt a tinge of regret at pursuing her friend's man but shook it off. Everyone on the planet was worried about themselves so why shouldn't she? "Hmph!"

*****

"What now, girl?" Reign asked as she snatched her door open without looking. Unique had just left so she assumed she doubled back to run her mouth some more. They were both good and high from multiple blunts courtesy of Bryan. Unique realized he broke bread quicker when she wore her little shorts, even with her big belly.

"Whata gwan?" Rankin asked from the doorway. Reign froze in fear and he took it as an invitation. He stepped inside and closed the door behind him.

"Sup, yo?" she asked when she came to. She shot a glance over to the pillow on the sofa with the pistol behind it.

"Mi came for see if err 'ting irie?" he asked and watched her ass shift under the T-shirt she wore as she made her way to the sofa.

"I'm good. I..." she began but paused when he dug into his pocket. She reached for the gun in case he came out with anything other than cash.

"Mi in the mood for love, ya know?" he said and ran his tongue over his black lips.

The cash in hand spoke for itself but so did Reign. She loved money but not enough to fuck him for it. "The doctor said, I can't have sex. The baby..." she said, hoping she could still get the money.

"You can suck 'pon it," he offered and gripped himself through his pants.

Reign grimaced and shivered at the thought. "Nah, homie. I don't suck no dick," she shot back, ready to shoot if he didn't take no for answer.

"Well, I'll have to suck that sweet pum-pum then," he said seductively and kneeled before her.

Curiosity led her to watch as he leaned in and licked her leg. He licked up and planted a kiss on her plump mound, right through her panties. Reign felt herself getting wetter as he munched on her cotton panties. It felt so good that she put up no resistance when he slid them aside and licked her lips.

"Ssss," she hissed when he twirled his tongue around her clit. Her legs spread wide so he could get to it. She stilled clutched the gun behind the pillow while he ate her out.

Rankin enjoyed sucking the young pussy and pulled out his dick. He spit some of her pussy juice on it for lube and began to stroke it. Reign remembered the video of her brother and Unique when a strange feeling began pulse through her body. She wasn't sure what was happening until it happened. Reign came so hard from her first orgasm that her whole body seized. Including the finger on the trigger behind the pillow.

Rankin thought he heard a muffled shot, like from a silencer, and the smell of gun smoke but he glanced up and saw both her hands. He couldn't worry about it now since he was about to bust.

"Blood fire!" he shouted and yanked harder on his dick. Reign watched with amazement as come erupted from the tip. Thick globs of semen shot up and landed on the sofa and coffee table.

"Mmm," Reign hummed when he stuck the tip of his tongue inside her as a going away present.

"Mi eat it until you 'ave ya pickney. Then me fuck you real good, ya know!" he cheered.

"Mm, can't wait!" she lied. She still had two more trimesters to go and would get as much out of him as she could. Even if she had to let him eat her out.

Rankin broke bread, then stood to leave. "Mi a fall true Saturday. Mi 'ave to meet Tito dem," he explained.

It was confirmation that Tito would be strapped with cash Friday night. Tito was about to get robbed.

# Chapter 3

"Girl, you crazy!" Unique said, shaking her head when Reign filled her in on Rankin's visit.

"Yup! Crazy and paid!" she said and showed off the money. "I just don't know what I'ma tell my moms about busting a shot through her sofa! Girl, I know he heard that shit but he was so open eating my cookie."

"What it feel like? When he ate you?" Unique asked seriously but Reign just twisted her face up. She had watched the video of her and Reef again after Rankin left to verify if she really came. She was pretty sure she felt the same feeling her friend felt on the video.

"I'm serious. I mean, only one guy ever did it, so I don't know if it was just him or..." She wanted to know. The little hood rats on the block often bragged about who ate them but neither Reign nor Unique really believed them. They would be lucky to get a dude to eat their cooking, let alone their coochie.

"I think that shit is good no matter who do it if they know what they doing. Cuz I damn sure ain't in love with him like you was with my brother. This blood clot said he gonna get me an apartment after I have the baby!" she laughed. "Said he gone leave his wife and err thing!"

"Shoot, one look and he gone know it ain't his. Kidd was light bright and he dark black!" Unique laughed. "Anyway, you ready for Friday?"

"I'm ready for Friday," Reign nodded. She had been asking herself that daily and decided she was. She was ready to kill someone. She was ready to kill several people actually but Tito would be first.

"Oh, and I ain't say it was your brother who ate me," Unique barely got out past the wide smile that said she was lying.

"You forgot I got his phone," she said and showed the video. Unique turned as red as her tan complexion would allow in embarrassment when she saw herself going down on Reef. The embarrassment didn't last long when she saw how pleased he was. Now she lifted her head in pride as Reef writhed in pleasure and went stiff.

"Dang, Neek! What that taste like?" Reign asked in a whisper. She always grimaced in disgust when she saw that part but Unique seemed proud.

"Like salty...snot," she laughed. The laughter subsided when she returned to the video and Reef dipped between her legs. "Okay, okay. That's enough."

"Yeah. I just found it on the chip. I was gonna erase it but figured you might want it," she said and shut it off.

"No, I mean, yes," she said and turned on her Bluetooth. Reign sent the video then deleted it from her phone. She'd seen it enough anyway so it was time to get rid of it.

"Man, I loved that dude!"

"Me too, yo. Me too!" Reign said and lit the next blunt.

*****

"You not working tonight, ma?" Reign asked when she saw her mother wasn't in uniform. In fact, she was looking quite cute and that was even more confusing. All she knew was that she needed her gone because she and Unique had a date with Tito. He was such a trick she and Unique tricked him into inviting them both up to his apartment later that night.

"No, I'm stepping out to meet a friend..." she said and left the rest hanging. She and Bryan had been talking on the phone all week and had agreed to meet up near the hospital. He had just left Simone's apartment and drove right by her building since she didn't let on that she lived on the same block.

"A date?" Reign dared as she looked her up and down. She looked good in the knee length skirt and tasteful blouse. Medium heels tilted her round ass slightly forward, adding to her appeal.

"Um, not really," she guessed since she wasn't exactly sure what to call it. She still wasn't sure what she was doing and backed out every couple of minutes. She had just decided to cancel and go pick up another shift at work. People were always getting shot, so they could definitely use another hand in the ER. Her phone rang and once again, it was on. "Hello? I'm on my way out the apartment now. Yes, I'm sure. Okay, how about 161st Street then? Okay. See you in a few."

"That is a date!" Reign insisted and pointed at the wide smile on her mother's face.

"Maybe, we'll see," Sharon blushed and giggled.

Reign hadn't seen that side of her since... Never.

"Just please use protection. We can't be looking crazy like Simone and Neek," she said. Now that both mother and daughter were showing, it looked just ghetto as can be.

"A date doesn't equal sex, young lady," she scolded. She covered her sexy with a large coat, hat and gloves and set out. It was too cold to wait on a bus so she hailed a taxi and was off for her date.

As soon as she left, Reign grabbed her phone to check in with Unique. "Sup yo? You ready for tonight?" she demanded.

"You ready?" she shot back since she was the one who had to do the dirty work.

"Hell yeah. My moms gone. Come on," she said and hung up.

"Yo ma, I'm going over to Reign's!" Unique called from the hallway assuming Bryan was still in her room. She was surprised when Simone opened the door and popped out of her door.

"You got weed?" she asked hopefully. "Bryant left and didn't leave me any money."

"Word?" Unique wondered since he'd slipped her a twenty when she arrived from school. "I'll bring some back."

"Okay. Thanks," she said and got back into her bed to Netflix and chill by herself.

Reign got an unexpected shock when she stepped outside and ran straight into Tito.

"Whoa, shorty. Where you off to? Thought you was coming over?" he asked. He made sure to look around so no one saw him.

"We are. I'm on my way to get Reign now. You got weed, right?" she asked, looking around for the same reason. She wouldn't want people saying she was the last person seen with him.

"Yeah, I got weed. I'm going up now, so come on," he urged and turned. He rushed into his building, rubbing his hands together like a greedy housefly ready to get into some shit. Unique took off and rushed up to Reign's apartment.

Reign snatched her door open as she came down the hall. "What he say?" Reign demanded as she snatched the door open and pulled her inside. She had, of course, been in her window and saw Tito push up on Unique.

"Nothing, just making sure we still coming. He all thirsty. Like he ain't just push me down!" she spat and rubbed the scab he'd made. "Get your coat so we can go!"

"Okay, mama, I'm coming," Reign snickered. She locked and loaded the pistol and checked the silencer once again. Both had new coats courtesy of Rankin's donation after eating Reign out. She'd split it with Unique and spent the rest the next day. She was ready for him to come again for both reasons.

"Let's walk around the block," Reign suggested when they stepped outside. They both knew someone was always in one of the thousand windows on the block so they didn't want to make a beeline to a murder scene.

"How 'bout we go to the end of the block and cross the street?" Unique replied when that New York cold nipped at her face.

They huddled up and walked down to Ogden before crossing over. A minute later, they walked into Tito's building. Time was in their favor and no one came or went as they went up the steps. Reign and

Unique stopped at his front door and locked eyes. They had a tacit talk to see if they would or could go through with it. Reign answered the unspoken question by lifting her hand and knocking on the door.

It was snatched open in an instant by a naked Tito.

"Come in!" Tito gushed. Both girls looked down at his erection and back up at each other. "Come on, yo!"

The girls shrugged and went inside. They saw lines of coke on the table and porn on the large flat screen. They also saw the bag he used to hold the re-up money. It was partially open and full of green bills so they shot each other a glance. Reign shook her head like 'this nigga dead'.

"Y'all get them clothes off!" he demanded and gave himself a few strokes. He'd snorted so much coke that he knew if he lost his erection it wouldn't be coming back.

"Chill, papi. Where the weed?" Reign said as she slid out of her coat but held on to it since it contained the gun.

"Oh yeah, roll up," he said, pointing at the pile of weed next to the coke. "Y'all want a line?"

"No!" they both blurted fearfully. They knew enough to know coke was a no-no. How any new people got hooked on the deadly drug after seeing so many people go out bad was beyond them. No one has ever seen a glamorous crackhead.

"Hurry up. I'm tryna fuck something! Who want they pussy ate first?" he asked, still pulling on his dick. Both girls raised their hand even though that's not what they came for. The porn on the TV had them both a little horny and Tito wasn't the least bit hard on the eye.

Reign caught up with herself and shook her head no. Neither Unique nor Tito saw since they were both caught up in their own adventures. He was tugging on his meat while she watched and rolled the blunt.

"Can I use your bathroom?" Reign asked.

"First door on the left," he said, pointing behind him with his free hand and jacking with the other.

Reign stood and set off with her coat. She stopped midway down the hall and pulled the pistol. Unique took her cue and spread her legs to distract him. Tito zeroed in on the plump pussy mound behind her sweats while Reign marched back and raised it to the back of his head.

"Shit, I'm 'bout to bust one!" Tito fussed as he neared an orgasm. He was full of coke and could go all night. He was so close to busting a nut but didn't make it.

*PST!* the silencer equipped gun whispered when it quietly sent a slug into his head. He died so quickly that he took two more strokes before he realized he was dead.

"Dang!" Unique exclaimed.

Tito's head dropped to his chest but his still gripped his dick tightly. They both inched forward to get a closer look. He almost looked asleep except for the hole in the back of his head leaking blood and brain matter.

"Come on, yo. Let's get this money!" Reign said and got in motion.

Unique began clearing the table by stuffing the weed and coke in the bag with the money. Reign rushed into his room to take everything she could find. She found more drugs, money and jewelry in his nightstand.

"He got a gun in here," Unique said when she came back. She remembered all the stuff he'd showed off when he had her here months back.

Tito was slumped on the sofa leaking while they cleaned him out. They hated to leave the thousands of dollars' worth of electronics but had no way of getting them home. Two pregnant girls moving a 65-inch TV would stand out like two pregnant girls moving a 65-inch TV.

"Okay. Go slow. Make sure no one see us," Reign warned when they reached his front door. She eased it open and peered down the hall.

The coast was clear so they eased out and hit the stairs. They quickly crossed the lobby towards the door when it suddenly opened. The old lady stopped dead in her tracks in fear but the girls ran right by her. They repeated their steps up to Ogden, crossed over and came back. Neither spoke or breathed till they were safely inside of Reign's apartment.

"Yo, we struck good!" Unique cheered as Reign emptied her pockets from what she'd found in his bedroom. She dumped it on her bed along with the contents of the bag. Reign nodded but didn't speak until she'd counted and split the money.

"Yo, that's like, eleven grand apiece!" she said, not counting the drugs. "That was a sweet lick!!"

*****

"You look nice," Bryan said once again when he helped Sharon out of his car. She looked great in the fitted scrubs she wore to work but even better dressed up.

"Thank you!" she giggled and fawned once again. It had been so long since she'd received a compliment from a man. The whistles and catcalls didn't count because she wasn't interested in those dudes. She was definitely interested in Bryan.

Sharon felt a nagging feeling at being on a date with her daughter's best friend's mother's man; but not enough to stop. He flashed his smile and she decided in an instant to fuck him. Why not when Simone bragged on the dick game and she hadn't had any in over ten years? She thought herself superior to Simone anyway so why not take her man? Why should Simone have a man and she not?

"What?" he had to ask of the mischievous grin on her face.

"Oh, nothing," she laughed, feeling her panties getting squishy.

They made flirty small talk all through dinner until it was time for dessert.

"Dessert?" Bryan asked, ready to spend a little extra in hopes of bending her over. He'd had to hold out on Simone so he could splurge a little on this new one. Unique still got broke off since he still wanted to break her off.

"At your place?" she asked and licked the salt from her margarita glass.

Bryan matched her wicked grin when he realized he was in. He mentally threw his arms in the air like he'd just won gold. Getting some new pussy is like winning a gold medal. "How about your place? I got a bunch of...people at mine," he said, meaning his wife and kids.

"Well, I live on the same block as your girlfriend, so..." Sharon said and smirked. She let out a giggle at the confused look on his face because she didn't know he was wondering which one. He went through quite a few girlfriends so she could have meant anyone.

"Huh?" he asked since that was safer. Let her explain instead of trying to explain and end up with his foot in his mouth and not his dick in her vagina.

"Um, Simone? On 164th. Our daughters are friends," she smiled.

"Reign?" he asked with a twinkle in his eye that should have been a red flag. Bryan had a thing for young girls.

"That's the one. So we don't have to play games. I'm a lonely lady and need some attention," she said with a slight growl that made Bryan's dick jump.

"We can get a room?" he said, nodding his head up and down as he stood.

"We can get a room," she agreed and nodded at the lump of wood in his pants. She accepted his hand as he rushed her back out to his car. The ride over to the Bronx was spent in silent thoughts.

Bryan was enthusiastic about some new pussy and plotted out which positions to put her in. She had a nice round ass so back shots was a must. She was pretty too so he had to let her ride so he could look up and look at her.

Sharon was pretty much thinking the same thing. It had been so long since she'd been with a man that she wasn't sure if she knew what to do. She had only been with two men in her life. A nasty stepdad who took what he wanted and her ex-husband who she gave all she had. She tensed when they crossed back over to the Bronx and passed her block.

"We're here," Bryan informed when they pulled to the motel.

Ironically, it was the same place where her daughter had lost her virginity and got impregnated. She let out a sigh and unbuckled the seatbelt.

Minutes later, they entered a rented room. Both ignored the smell of smoke and moved in for a kiss. Bryan felt her knees buckle when he slid his tongue in her mouth. She felt a gush of juice soak her panties and was ready to have him inside of her. Sharon broke the kiss off and stepped out of her shoes. Bryan watched as she pulled her blouse off and dropped her dress.

"Wow!" he said, seeing her fine brown frame in a matching black panty and bra set. Her flat stomach and plump breasts made his dick jump and reminded him to remove his own clothes.

Sharon was wowed as well when he stepped out of his clothes. He was in good shape from lifting gurneys all day, every day. She was relieved to see a normal sized dick when he removed his boxers. Her ex-husband was above average and it took birthing two kids before she could enjoy him without the pain.

They both went around the large bed and met in the middle. Their kisses picked up where they'd left off as they groped each other.

"Sss!" Sharon hissed when his hand reached between her legs.

He wanted to hiss too when he felt how wet and slippery she was. "Let's get these off!" he said and urgently removed her panties while she removed her bra. She lifted her hips to help him with his task.

Men usually start with the lips, neck and breasts as they go down on a woman but Bryan couldn't wait. He dove face first between her legs and attacked with his twirling tongue. Sharon came almost instantly.

"Damn!" he laughed with a wet face when she finished shivering and shaking from an intense orgasm.

"Don't laugh! I haven't been with a man in over ten years," she admitted.

That made Bryan even harder and he climbed up to enter her. He looked down to watch as he worked the head of his dick between her slippery lips. He added a little pressure and slowly sank inside of her. She winced and grabbed the sheets as he entered her.

He stuck his tongue back in her mouth and searched for his stroke. He would usually shove himself inside Simone and pound until they both came but Sharon was different. They locked eyes, traded kisses and made love. Not for long, though, because she was too tight, too pretty and her soft whimpers soon overwhelmed him. Dudes usually remember the rubbers they forgot to put on right before they come. There's always time to pull out if they want to. He didn't want to and instead pushed deep inside of her.

"Un uh," she said and gently pushed him up.

"My bad, I..." he said and pulled out.

He was still rock hard and it was too late anyway so she reached down and guided him back inside of her.

They made love for the rest of the night.

# Chapter 4

164th Street was buzzing on a busy Saturday morning as the night people traded places with the day people. The junkies swapped out with the working folk and the older dealers gave it over to the younger ones. Sharon arrived in a cab so Simone wouldn't see their man dropping her off. Simone had been calling his phone more than his wife so he swung by there before he went home.

He was just as sprung on Sharon as she was on him and they both knew this was the beginning of a thing. A thing that could not possibly end well. She saw him pull up at Simone's building and lifted her head. Not necessarily in pride but more like 'I don't give a fuck'. She lifted her head high enough to look right over her own bullshit and went inside. She had done everything right in life and what did that get her? A dead son, a pregnant daughter and a mountain of bills. She deserved a little happiness; even with someone else's man.

"Ma?" Reign asked almost fearfully when she heard the door open and close. She felt nothing about killing Tito but kept expecting police to come knocking. The first murder is always like that. She'd get used to it because there would certainly be more.

"It's me, baby," Sharon sang. She was pleasantly sore between her legs but still had a song in her heart.

"Are you just getting in?" Reign reeled with a hand on her hip as if she was the adult.

"Yes. My friend and I stayed up talking all night," she replied. It wasn't a lie because 'fuck me' and 'I'm coming' is technically talking and she'd said both all night long.

"Oh, okay. Me and Neek ain't do nothing. We just..." she said but her mother was walking away and entered her room. She looked out the window to see if Tito had been discovered yet. All she saw was Seven and the other dope boys milling about in front of his building.

***

"He still ain't answer?" Seven asked when Lil Stevie came back from trying his luck. Everyone was waiting around to pay what they owed so they could re-up.

Tito ran the trap the same way Reef did and fronted the work out to the young boys. They got to keep thirty off each hundred they sold. All debts had to be settled before Saturday when the dread came to collect and supply the block. If not you would get beat up and cut off. The latter hurt more than the former because no one else was hiring.

"Nah, yo," he said and scratched his head. He needed more weed so he wasn't going anywhere. He sat on the stoop and waited like everyone else.

"Probably got some pussy up there," Seven guessed since Tito was quite the playboy. He had no idea that his playing days were over.

Unique stepped out of her building and glanced over to what would soon be a crime scene. She snapped her face away when she saw Seven and marched over to Reign's.

"Sup yo?" Reign greeted when she opened the door for her friend. She could feel the cold emanating off of her but still asked, "Cold out there?"

"It's winter in New York. Of course it's cold outside!" she shot back and made a face to show what she thought of the silly question.

"Guess we gonna have to catch a cab then," Reign announced since they were officially ballers now. Each had over eleven grand in cash and a couple pounds apiece of weed, not to mention a pile of slum jewels that they could sell once they ran through their cash.

"Word!" Unique cheered since she was with it. She realized she was a little loud and asked, "Where's yo mom?"

"Ooh, moms got her groove on last night! Came in an hour ago talking 'bout all they did was talk all night!" Reign laughed

"Girl, my moms and dude going at it too, I bet. He just came in, too!" Unique said.

Once Reign was bundled up, they headed out to go blow their money.

Both girls shot a glance over to Tito's building as they stepped out. There was still no police so they headed up to Ogden to hail a taxi.

"Where to?" the Spanish driver asked, expecting them to say 161st Street since most of his fares did. The short trip only paid a couple of bucks but enough of them each day paid the bills.

"Fordham Road," they said together.

The driver turned all the way around to see if they could afford the long trip. He squinted his eyes and asked, "Tu tiene dinero?"

"Hell yeah we got money, my nigga!" Unique shot back and whipped out a wad of colorful bills.

"He just tried us!" Reign added and pulled hers too.

They both were happy to have a reason to show off all their cash and now they did. They still cursed the driver out the whole way uptown. He didn't mind as long as he got paid. He turned up the salsa music and tuned them out until he put them out on Fordham and the Grand Concourse.

They set off down the hill to spend every penny they had.

\*\*\*

"Man, did any one see this nigga leave?" Seven asked out of pure frustration. He hadn't left the front of the building and Tito's car hadn't moved.

"Nah," someone replied and sighed.

"Man," Seven said and stood. It was never too cold to sell dope but it was way too cold to be sitting outside and not selling it so he went inside and tried his luck again.

Seven reached Tito's door once again but this time he leaned his ear against the door before he knocked. He heard the sounds of sex but he had that same dvd and knew it wasn't live.

"Ayo, Tito!" he called out and knocked loudly on the heavy steel door. Still no reply, so he tried his luck and tried the doorknob. It turned easily but he let it go and called his name once more. "Tito! We all outside, yo!" Seven's knuckles hurt from knocking so he turned the knob once more and pushed it open.

"Ayo, Tito, we all... Oh shit!" he said, seeing Tito on the sofa staring off into the afterlife. He'd seen enough dead bodies in his short life to know this was one.

He wasn't sure what was going on so he pulled his hammer from his waist. His mentor Reef always said, "When in doubt, grab your gun." He moved quickly and quietly through the apartment and made sure it was empty. Now it was time to get down to business.

"Okay, first of all, you won't be needing this," he informed the corpse as he removed the chunky chain from his neck. It was crusted with dried blood but it would come right off. Same with the bracelet on his wrist. He got to keep the rings since his hand was still on his dick.

Another search of the apartment explained the hole in his head since there was no cash or drugs anywhere in sight. There was that big ass TV along with other electronics. He pulled a sheet off the bed and loaded clothes and sneakers in it. He checked the hall before dragging all he could up to the roof and stashing it for later. Once he was done, he rushed back down to join the rest.

"He up there?" Rufus asked when he returned and took his seat.

"Nah. Still no answer. I'm about to get me a slice," he said and popped back up. He heard people asking him to bring them one back too but didn't answer. Instead, he ordered his food and stepped back out. He looked around a moment before using the payphone to call 911.

"911, what's your emergency?" a stoic operator asked. She took down the address as he reported the murder.

***

"Girl, wait til we have these babies. We gonna be the baddest bitches on the block!" Reign cheered since that was really important to her. They only bought sweats for maternity clothes but built their post-delivery wardrobes.

"Word," Unique replied with a lot less enthusiasm. Being fly was important enough but she still wanted to get the hell away from 164th. The Bronx and New York even. But that seemed impossible at the moment, especially with the way they blew their money. They barely had enough to catch a cab back to the block, so how could they escape New York?

"Oh, okay! Rich bitch shit!" Neta shouted when she saw the girls pull up in a cab and begin unloading bags.

"Y'all know Reign got a rich baby daddy!" Jewel said sarcastically. The joke was that Rankin was so ugly that it wasn't even worth having his baby to get his money. Everyone knew Jewel could actually be pregnant by anyone on the block so Reign let it slide.

"Help us get this stuff upstairs. We got weed," Unique said and her friends were hired. They all grabbed a bag and headed inside. Reign played the back to make sure no one eased off.

"I don't even want to know," Sharon said and shook her head when the caravan of clothing came into the apartment. The girl shopped non-stop but never worked a day in her life.

"Did you cook?" Reign asked sweetly but it was a swipe. Her mother had been drunk for weeks so she wanted to rub it in.

"Actually, I did but not enough for everyone," she said since the rest of the crew was here. She always made sure she made enough for Unique but not the crew.

"Oh, they not staying. We about to go over to Neek's," she said, leaving off the part about smoking weed once they got there.

They all headed out and headed over to Unique's building. She only took one bag of clothes to wear now and left the wear later clothes over there so her mother wouldn't take them. A few dope boys milled around Tito's since the cops still hadn't shown up.

"Where you get money from?" Simone demanded and pulled Unique's bag from her hand to see what she had. She twisted her lips at the big granny panties and sweats.

"From her."

"From me," she and Reign said at the same time just like they'd rehearsed.

"Y'all ain't get me nothing?" she pouted. Today was a bad day since Bryan didn't have any dough or dick for her.

"Of course!" Unique said and split her haul with her. "And we got weed!"

"Roll up then!" the bad parent cheered. She turned on the radio so they could chill and get high.

They sparked the first blunt as the first cop car pulled on the block.

***

"Po-po," Rufus warned when a cop car pulled onto the block.

No one had drugs so they didn't have to run. They did move along when the car pulled to stop in front of the building they were waiting in front of.

"That's right, scatter like the little roaches you'se are," the cop riding shotgun teased.

"Let's just check this dead body call so we can get some food," the driver said. He put the car in park and led the way inside. "Would be a damn walk up!"

"Of course," his partner said and they hoofed up the stairs.

"Try the knob so we can get out of here," the driver said after banging with his flashlight. To both their surprise, it opened.

Both cops looked at the corpse then each other. Slow smiles spread on both faces since they were the first to arrive. They eased in and began to collect whatever they could find of value. Poor Tito got robbed for a third time before they called it in.

"Fuck they got going on?" Seven asked as he came on the scene. He was mad he'd left things for the cops to take but happy that they didn't go up to the roof.

"I'on know," one of the dope boys replied and shrugged.

Soon homicide and the coroner was on the scene.

"Something going on out there!" Simone said when she peeped out the window.

All the girls rushed over to get a look then piled out the door to get an even closer look. No one wants secondhand gossip.

Reign and Unique shared a glance and followed the herd. They took their places in the crowd and watched as Tito was carried out in a body bag.

"Uh oh, here come the drama!" someone announced when Lisa came out of her building.

"Oh hell no! Somebody gotta tell me something!" she demanded and got in people's faces. The police didn't even bother asking anyone anything since no one answered.

"We been waiting all day for big bruh but he ain't came out. Then Po-po showed up," Seven offered. That's all she was getting out of him so he walked off and left her.

"I'ma find out!" she shouted to the departing crowd. The show was over so everyone moved on to wait for the next one. One thing for sure is— there was always a next one.

# Chapter 5

"Well, I'm off to work," Sharon said with a lonely sigh. In a perfect world, she would be on her back, legs open and Bryan deep inside of her. This wasn't a perfect world so she had to catch a bus to a train and go to work.

"Okay..." Reign said and waited for the usual list of 'don't do this' and 'don't do that' but none came. Sharon gave up when her daughter turned up pregnant. Everything else paled in comparison so she kept it to herself.

Reign got into the window to watch her mother to the bus stop but something else caught her eye and stole her attention. Rankin slowly pulled on the block. She tried to pull away but he looked up and looked directly at her. He cracked an ugly smile and winked an ugly eye with his ugly ass.

There was still a congregation in front of Tito's building as the dope boys milled around trying to figure out their next move. A dope boy with no dope turns into a jack boy and nobody wants that. Niggas are going to eat no matter who they have to eat.

"Whata gwan. Where Tito dem?" Rankin asked as he pulled up to a stop in front of the building. He knew from the long faces before they even opened their mouths.

"Dead,yo. But I got this now. I'ma hold the block down now," Seven said and stuck his chest out. He wasn't the oldest but no one objected to his claiming the throne. Heavy is the head that wears the crown and most niggas don't want them problems. The last three kings had all had packed funerals. The two before them were serving from now on upstate and the three before them died, too. Nah, no one wants those problems.

"You?" Rankin snarled and looked him up and down. Seven looked straight ahead like a soldier at inspection. "You 'ave mi money?"

"Yeah. How much we owe?" he said. Everyone was present and knew there was a tab to keep the flow of weed flowing. Everyone except Mike-Mike's shady ass. He was here earlier to pay up but decided to keep it once they carted Tito away in a bag.

"Ten 'tousand dollar!" the dread said like it was a million. He twisted his lips as the dope boys handed the youth their money. Seven added his and counted it up.

"Eight bands. I'll get the rest," he said and handed it over. Rankin and the dope boys frowned but for different reasons. The dread didn't like being shorted and the dope boys doubted Seven could come up with two bands. They hustled like he did and most didn't have two hundred. Mainly because they were tricks and tricked off their money on weed, clothes, sneakers and pussy. Who could blame them really when life could end at any moment so they lived for the moment? This was the Bronx, after all. Sex, money, murder.

"Hmp?" Rankin huffed and looked him up and down once more. "You 'ave 'tirty minute, ya know."

"I don't need that long," Seven smiled as the dread turned and walked away.

"Ooh, girl, he coming your way!" Unique warned on the phone when Rankin turned and crossed over.

"I see his bumba clot ass. I got something for his ass if he come up here!" she growled. She was fronting, though, because her pussy jumped just thinking about him sucking on it. She still stuck the pistol behind the sofa pillow and waited.

The super had the heat booming so she had her T-shirt and panties on already. She reached down and removed the panties in case he wanted to eat her out again, like unwrapping a piece of candy. He was still going to pay for what he did but she still planned to get every coin out of him that she could while she could because dead men don't pay well.

"Want me to come?" Unique asked and rolled off her bed to roll out. Their superintendent was stingy with the heat so she was already dressed.

"No! I mean, no. I'm straight," she shouted, then caught herself.

Unique caught her too and started laughing. "Girl, you too much!" she giggled. She heard the knock on the door and Reign checked out.

"I'll hit you back," she said and ended the call. She walked over to the door and called, "Who?"

"Rude mon dem," Rankin said in an attempt to sound sexy. He actually did but it disintegrated the second she opened the door and saw his face.

"Oh, hey," she greeted and turned away like a person does when they look at the sun. His ugly was just like the sun and burned the eye if you looked directly at it. Most people wore shades in his presence to dim the ugly.

"Mmm," he said, watching her round cheeks as she walked away. It was way bigger than before since she was way bigger from the baby. "Mi bring a little something for ya," he said, extending a fistful of dollars. The thousand in dope boy money looked like more since it was every denomination the treasury printed. He deliberately wrapped the tens and twenty with two hundreds and stuffed it with fives and ones.

"The doctor said I still can't fuck," she advised before reaching for the money.

"No problems. You want rude mon to suck 'pon it?" he asked.

Her vagina answered first with a throb a gush of juice. "I still ain't gone suck pon you back!" she demanded and twisted her face up.

He was cool with it since he'd bedded plenty of young girls before they started sucking dick. It was just a matter of time and he was patient. "No problems, mon. Turn around," he said and Reign complied. She turned around on the sofa and bent over so she could reach her gun. Rankin flipped her T-shirt over her pretty round ass and shook his head. "Lawda mercy!"

Rankin marveled at the young ass with the swollen vagina hanging between. It looked so good that he didn't know where to start. He did know his dick was way too hard to be stuck in his pants. He unbuckled his pants and set the raging erection free. He gripped it with one hand and kneeled down to eat his meal.

"Un uh," Reign moaned in confusion when he flicked his tongue on her anus. It felt good and wrong at the same time. Rankin twirled his tongue around it once more before dropping to the dripping pussy. "Sss!"

Rankin gulped down a mouthful of juice then sucked 'pon that sweet pum-pum like a mango. He peeled her ass cheek open with one hand and licked and lapped while tugging on his dick.

"Ugh!" he grunted and busted a nasty nut all over her leg and the sofa. She was repulsed from the hot cum on her leg but too close to busting a nut of her own to complain.

"Ssss, shit, shit, sss," she hissed, cussed and came right behind him. Rankin put a cherry on top by slipping back up and rimming her anus once more. All she could do was grip the pillows and hold on. Hold on and think of what to spend the money on.

"Go for seconds, no?" he asked and rolled her onto her back.

"Go for seconds, yes!" she agreed and spread her legs wide. Rankin attacked with that twirling tongue while pulling on himself. Reign grabbed handfuls of knotty dreads and pulled his face into her pussy. He probed inside with his tongue until she came again.

"Mi turn!" he grunted and pulled frantically on his dick.

Reign leaned up and watched as he exploded on her thighs. She was repulsed and amazed at the same time.

"You gotta go. Before my moms..." she said.

"Okay. Mi ah go now," he said and put his big dick back into his pants. "What you know 'bout da 'yout dem called Seven? 'Im good? Ya brudda mess with 'im?"

"Seven, yeah, he solid. My brother messed with him the long way," she said, knowing why he asked and that she'd just gotten him a promotion. That meant the pretty thug owed her one. He could have gotten her cherry had he been patient. He ended up in her best friend and that crushed that crush. Friends don't fuck behind friends, no matter how cute the boy is.

Reign stood and wobbled on rubbery legs and let Rankin out. She had just locked the multiple locks when another knock came. She looked out the peephole and shook her head before taking the locks back off.

"Girl..." Unique said, shaking her head too, "look at you!"

"What?" Reign asked as if her hair wasn't all over the place and face wasn't flushed. "Girl, he ate my ass. Gave me a band and ate my ass!"

"Wish someone would give me a band to eat my ass," Unique pouted and plopped on the sofa. The wrong spot on the sofa as she felt something on her hand. "What the.... Eww!"

"Girl, he be jacking off while he be eating me," she explained then felt a sudden urge to shower so she could wash his seed of her legs. "Roll up, I'll be right back."

Unique shrugged and rolled a blunt from the supplies left on the table. She entertained herself by looking out the window to see Rankin pull back up on Seven and the rest of the dope boys.

"You 'ave mi money?" was all Rankin wanted to know when he reached the crew. He directed his speech to Seven since he'd stepped up with his chest out. Seven replied by extending the two thousand they were short. His friends squinted at him and wondered how he had that much money. Little did they know, he had ten more grand in his room. He preferred to stack his instead of blowing it as soon as he got it. His good looks more than made up for his lack of etceteras. He had enough clothes and sneakers for a decent rotation and a large gold 7 hanging from a gold chain. The rest got put up for rainy days sure to come.

"Come. Let mi 'ave a word wit you, ya know," the dread said and hit the key fob to unlock his doors.

Seven followed and got in on the passenger seat. "What's up, yo?" Seven asked although he already knew. His chicken chest was still poked out even while seated.

"You the man now," he said and pulled the bag of weed from the backseat.

Seven nodded as the dread laid out the rules and consequences for violations of those rules. Seven agreed and sealed the deal with eye contact and a handshake. He reminded the dread of Reef in that way.

Seven got out to take the work home but saw Lisa coming out of her building. He needed to talk to her too since he wanted the coke connect as well. The weed was cool to keep change in one's pocket but coke was it. It would finance his dreams of getting out of the Bronx. He'd spent a few summers down south and had fallen in love with the peace and quiet of the country. He had plans and dreams but they all played out in South Carolina.

"Yo, Lisa, can I holla at you real quick?" he asked as she approached.

"Nah, little nigga," she scoffed and hopped into Rankin's passenger seat before he pulled off.

"Whata gwan?" Rankin asked, wondering what was going on. He knew her as Reef's ex and the Tito's cousin but neither explained why she was in his car.

Lisa had lost another meal ticket and decided to eat some dick to get another. She explained herself by reaching over for his zipper. Rankin watched her remove his flaccid dick and lean down. She planted a loud kiss on the fat head then twirled her tongue around it. It was flaccid no more and she took him down to her larynx.

"Blood fire!" he cheered and leaned back to enjoy that neck and throat. He'd just gotten off twice so she was going to have to work for it.

And work she did, with all she had until she had a mouthful of Jamaican cum. She swallowed loudly for effect and held him in her mouth until he went soft.

"Now that I have your attention," she giggled with cum on her breath. "My cousin is gone but I'm here. Let me handle the business. I helped Reef and Tito. I know the whole operations. Plus, I got some bomb ass head," she said, laying out her case.

"A gal dem?" he asked curiously. He was a true chauvinist and believed women were only good for what she just did. "I put the 'yout dem Seven in charge,"

"Seven?" she reeled and recalled just chumping him off. She realized the bag he had was that bag and she'd just sucked the wrong dick.

"Go long now. Mi 'ave ta go," he said, shooing her out of his car by hitting the locks. She realized the only thing she was getting out of him was in her belly so she hopped out.

Lisa always was and always will be a hoe so she held her hoe head high and marched over to Seven's building. His elevator opened and she rode up to his floor. She marched down the hall and knocked on his door.

"Chill, yo. I just got... Huh?" he said when he opened the door. He was expecting the dope boys in search of work but found the thot instead

Lisa pushed him back inside and closed the door behind him. She dropped down and sucked her third dick of the day. An apple a day may keep the doctor away but she sucked dick to keep poverty at bay. Fuck being broke so she sucked dick until she choked.

"Yoooo!" Seven cheered at the grown lady head. The young girls his age had just started sucking dicks and weren't very good at it yet. Lisa showed out by putting her hands behind her back and giving him all neck. The teen didn't stand a chance against a pro hoe head game. "Argh!"

"I'm your girl now. You can get that err day. Plus this bomb ass pussy," she informed. "Oh, and here go Tariq number. I'll let him know you gonna call."

"Um, okay?" he agreed and scratched his head. "Wait, I got a girlfriend. Jewel. She pregnant, too."

"Well...now you got two!" she insisted and turned to leave.

Seven was stuck for seven seconds before he shrugged and got to work bagging up the work.

The crew was waiting when he finally made it back downstairs. Of course they were since they needed work. Seven picked up right where Tito left off and supplied the dope boys. All except Mike-Mike that is since he didn't want to pay what he owed.

"What about me?" Mike-Mike whined when Seven finished up.

"What about you? You ain't even kick in what you owed to keep shit going. I know you got bread so if you wanna shop, I'll let you get it at cost but I ain't fronting you a crumb," he said emphatically.

"It's like that?" he dared dangerously.

"It's just like that!" Seven dared back. There was a brief standoff that ended with Mike-Mike reaching into his pocket and coming out with cash. He glared maliciously as they traded dope for dollars.

It was a victory for Seven but he was too young and too green to understand he'd just made an enemy.

# Chapter 6

"I'm out, Neek. Hold down the noise cuz my man in there sleeping," Simone said, totally contradicting herself. If Bryan were truly her man, she wouldn't have had to catch the bus to stand at a register for eight hours. Even if she did have to work, he could at least drive her instead of sleeping, if he was truly her man.

"A'ight, ma," she said, pretending to whisper.

As soon as she left, Unique stretched out on the sofa to watch TV. A few minutes later, Bryan came out of the bedroom. Bryan was shirtless and had a lump in his sweat pants from prepping himself with a few strokes.

"Did you mom leave already?" he asked while scanning her legs.

"Pss, this nigga just tried me," Unique mumbled to herself. He'd tried her so she tried him right back. "Can I have some money?"

"Sure. What you need, pretty girl?" he asked and sat next to her feet. She pulled her legs up a little and he zoomed in between her thighs. The poof of hair on her young vagina made it look fatter than it really was.

"Like a band, I mean a thousand dollars. Need stuff for my baby," she said and closed her legs to end the show.

"Whoa, I can't afford all that! I have a wi... Um, no, that's a bit much," he said, catching himself before revealing he had a wife and kids, not to mention another date coming up with Sharon. He would gladly have paid if he had it if it got him inside of her.

"Okay," Unique shrugged. She still had a few grand from the Tito lick so she wasn't pressed. Unique turned her attention back to the TV while he focused on her legs.

"You ever had your pussy ate?" he asked, assuming that she hadn't. Most young guys didn't eat pussy yet so chances were she hadn't and that would be his way in.

"Yup," she said without turning from the TV. "I never had my ass ate, though,"

"Hmp?" he huffed since he never ate ass himself. He looked down at the invisible line and decided to cross it. "Want me to?"

"Want you to what? Eat my ass? And you got my moms pregnant?" she pressed and finally faced him.

"Huh? No! I was saying, you want me to cook? You hungry? Eating for two, you know!" he rambled and back peddled.

"I'm good, yo," she declined and hefted herself off the sofa. She walked away but whipped her head around to catch Bryan staring at her ass. She shook her head and continued on to her room. After getting fully dressed, she stepped back out. She held her head high and marched over to Reign's.

Unique noticed the block was booming when she walked outside. Seven kept the crack trade to the end of the block but that wasn't far enough. Crackheads still roamed day and night looking for something to smoke or something to steal that they could sell for something to smoke.

*****

"Wait, he said what?" Reign frowned. "That nigga tried you up! You should tell yo moms!"

"Yo, my moms is so damn sprung she probably won't believe me," she said, twisting her lips wistfully. "Shoulda recorded his ass!"

"Shoulda? Should! Next time he come at you like that, record it. Prop your phone up just like when you gave my brother some head," Reign snickered.

"Whatever. You right, though. That's exactly what I should do but..." she paused to think about the possible consequences.

"But Simone ain't gonna care. She might still blame you cuz she don't wanna lose her man," Reign answered. The room went silent as they both retreated inside their heads and searched for solutions. A finger snap snapped the silence when she found one. "Record his ass and we gonna blackmail him!"

"Yup!" Unique agreed and nodded. She lit a blunt and proceeded to get high. High and horny, she checked the clock. Simone wouldn't be home for hours. She checked out the window and saw Bryan's car still parked. She stood and announced, "I'm out."

"A'ight yo. Holla back," Reign said and chucked deuces with one hand and reached for the remote with the other.

Unique waved at Neta and the other girls out in the cold and kept it moving. She entered her apartment and then her room. After propping the phone up, she checked the angle and lighting and dressed down to her gown. The web was set so she went to get the fly.

"Yes?" Bryan called in response to the knock on Simone's door. He was getting dressed to go home for a few hours but that got put on hold when he saw the big pregnant thighs under the gown and big pregnant breasts poking through it.

"You still wanna eat my ass?" she asked bluntly.

"I, I, I, um, I was saying you want me, I, I mean..." he stuttered and stammered.

"If you gonna do it, come on. We can't do it in here," she said and turned to leave.

Bryan looked at that big pregnant ass and had to have it. "Shit..." he said and took his clothes back off. He stripped down to his boxers rushed down the hall and knocked on her cracked door.

"Hey, Mr. Bryan. What's up?" she asked innocently. She was innocently under her comforter like she had been sleep.

"You know what I want!" he said and closed the door behind him. His erection poked out in his drawers as he snatched the comforter away from her legs.

"What, are you... doing?" she pleaded for the camera.

"Turn over," he answered and flipped her over. He pulled her up on her hands and knees and shook his head at her pretty vagina hanging between her thighs. It soaked his fingers the second he touched it. "Shit!"

"Shit!" she agreed when he leaned in and flicked his tongue on her anus. She almost collapsed but Bryan gripped her hips to hold her in place.

"What, are you, doing?" she moaned as he ran his tongue from her vagina to her asshole. Both felt great but he couldn't answer because his tongue was busy twirling. She figured it out when she busted a nut in his mouth.

"Man, fuck this!" Bryan said to himself. He had said he would just eat her and not fuck her but that was before all that juice gushed out the sweet, young box. It was so tight when he stuck his finger in it, how could he not stick his dick in it?

Unique had no plans to have sex with him but made no objections when he dropped his drawers and kneeled behind her. She forgot all about the recording when he rubbed his dick head between her lower lips, all slippery and wet. Her back arched instinctively as he began to ease inside, body language for 'get this pussy'.

"Ssss," she moaned in a mix of pleasure and pain as he inched inside, inch by inch.

"Damn!" Bryan cursed when he felt how tight she was. Her mother and his own wife were nowhere near as tight. Sharon was almost this tight but not quite. These and other thoughts crossed through his mind but couldn't prevent him from busting a quick nut. She was already pregnant so he pushed in and let go. "Damn it, man!"

"Dang," Unique giggled as he wiggled and writhed inside of her. Most dudes had that reaction when they got inside of her. Reef was the only one who lasted long enough to make her cum too.

"Next time, I'ma really get it good," he vowed and pulled out of her. He leaned down and kissed her ass cheek and got up. He waddled away with his drawers down so he could wash his dick in the sink.

"Mmm, shit!" Unique moaned, then remembered the camera. She rolled off and stopped the video. "Got yo dumb ass!"

"Hey..." Bryan said when he returned and stuck his head in the door. "It's not a thousand but..."

"Thank you," she said and accepted his offering. The hundred dollars might just get her through a weekend with the way she blew money. She and Reign were running through Tito's money at an amazing rate and he wasn't even in the ground yet.

"Our secret, right?" he checked like he always did. Only this time, she had a box full of his seeds.

"Our secret," she giggled and cooed like a little girl as he backed away. Her lips twisted as soon as he closed the door. "Like I would really tell my moms you ate my ass!"

\*\*\*\*\*

"Get it, get it! Mmhm, get it!" Lisa moaned behind her as Seven dug her out doggy style. She called him over to meet the coke connect but gave him a side order of some good, hot, Puerto Rican pussy. Arroz con pollo don't have shit on some good Latina pussy.

All he could do was hold on and hump for his dear life. He could hardly believe he was inside the baddest chick on the block. He'd actually fantasized about her many a day and the reality was wetter and hotter than he expected. So wet and hot that he couldn't hang.

"Shit!" he fussed and tried to pull out.

"Nuh uh," Lisa laughed to herself as she grabbed him and held him inside. She clamped her box tight shut on him. She could feel him pulsating inside of her as he pumped her full of young boy cum.

Lisa recalled Reef speaking highly of the youth and his grind. He would be out there hustling while his counterparts shopped and tricked off their money. He knew he lived with a barely spry grandmother who could do nothing more than keep a roof over his head. Beyond that, he was on his own.

"What you did that for?" he asked, sounding just as naïve as she took him for. He wasn't the biggest fan of rubbers but had a mean pull out game. He was still scratching his head about Jewel popping up pregnant. He smoked a lot of weed but still didn't recall busting in her.

"Don't worry about it, papi. No more babies coming out this pussy," she said and pushed him up. All she fucked was dope boys so it wouldn't really matter which one knocked her up. All she knew was she needed to get a baby in her, ASAP. Somebody had to take care of her.

"Pull your pants up. Tariq will be here in a minute."

"Okay," he said nervously. He had asked around and prices were nine hundred an ounce and nowhere near as good as what Reef was getting. Tito got the connect next and the quality stayed the same. He wished he had time to wash all the good juice from his dick but Lisa's phone buzzed with Tariq's arrival.

"He's here!" she relayed and pulled her panties back on to keep the cum from running out and down her leg.

"Bet," Seven said and checked his clothes.

A minute later, Lisa answered the knock on her door. "Hey, papi," she greeted and tried to kiss Tariq's cheek. Seven noticed he grimaced and pulled away.

"What's good, yo? He next?" Tariq asked with a head nod towards Seven. He recognized the face from the trap. Every time he came to the block, Seven was trapping. He never sweated him or his car when he rolled through.

"He next," Lisa said and Seven stuck his chest out again and nodded.

"Let's take a ride youngin," Tariq said and turned to leave.

Lisa opened her mouth to protest but snapped it shut just as quickly. Seven would fill her in when he got back even if she had to suck it out of him. Seven still hadn't spoken as he followed him out of the apartment. They hit the steps and saw someone's dog had just taken a fresh dump on the landing.

"Grab that, youngin," Tariq said, nodding toward the pile of doggy doo.

"Nah, B. What I want some shit for?" he shot back.

"Ask yo self that. You just stuck yo dick in some shit, so..." he said as they crossed the lobby.

Seven nodded in reply and understood. "Word," he agreed and cut Lisa off in his mind. He had wanted to fuck her and he did so now, "Fuck her."

Seven never sweated Tariq's BMW when it came through the block but he sure sweated it when he got in the passenger seat. It was fitting since his peers sweated him for pulling off with the connect. Some were proud he was about to be the connect. One was seething in jealousy and envy as Mike-Mike snarled at them.

"You want one of these?" Tariq asked, seeing Seven looking around the car like a Times Square tourist.

"Nah, it's dope but, nah. I'ma buy a barbershop. And a restaurant, and a..." Seven said, laying out his plans. The smart kid once calculated how many customers came through the pizza shop in an hour. He multiplied how much they spent and multiplied that but the twelve hours they were open. The pizza shop made as much money as the connect but didn't have to run when the cops came.

Tariq nodded in agreement with the kid's dreams and goals. Especially when he mentioned South Carolina. He'd once dreamed of escaping New York but the money started flowing and he couldn't leave it. He was trapped by the trappings of success and knew it. His fate would be prison or the cemetery and there was nothing he would do to stop it.

"So you ready to run yo block?" Tariq dared and turned to face him as he drove.

"I'm ready. I already got the weed; I just need a good price on the coke," he replied confidently.

"How's about five hundred an ounce?" he shot back and the car went quiet as Seven mentally did the math.

He could make a little over two thousand dollars off each ounce and pay the dope boys thirty bucks off each hundred, which was six hundred, minus the five hundred equaled eleven hundred which netted him nine hundred an ounce times the ten ounces he planned to buy and he would net nine thousand from this deal times doing it four times a week and...

"Shit!" Seven shouted at his newfound riches. He needed a good six month run and he would be straight.

"I know, right?" Tariq laughed since he'd correctly guessed what the kid was doing inside his head. He drove over to a Harlem pizza shop where the Italian workers greeted him like royalty. They ordered a few slices and ate at the counter.

"Thanks, Tariq!" the clerk said and gave a handshake instead of a bill.

"No problem, B," he said and led the way back to his car.

"Them dudes fuck with you, huh?" Seven said in awe.

"Of course. That's my shop. They work for me!" Tariq said proudly. It let Seven know he was on the right track. His street dreams went far beyond the streets. They chopped it up on the ride back over to the Bronx and completed the first sale.

"Five bands. You can count it," Seven said, paying for his first ten ounces.

Tariq stared at the money for a second since the price he gave was for half a brick and up. He had no doubt the kid would get his weight up so he took the money. "You'll rock with my man Quan from now on," he said and passed off the coke and phone number. "You got a lieutenant, yet?"

"Um..." Seven paused to see who he could trust. "Benji, I guess."

"Good, cuz kings don't seem to live long on your block."

# Chapter 7

"Un uh, girl!" Reign shrieked as Unique giggled while showing her the recording of Bryan eating her out from the back. "You was just supposed to record him saying it, not actually doing it!"

"I know but when he said it, I got horny!" she admitted. "Girl, I can't front. That shit felt good! He put his tongue all in me!"

"I see!" Reign said as the Unique on the screen screeched and came.

"Okay, okay. That's enough!" Unique said and scrambled to stop the recording. Reign frowned curiously at her urgency and knew something was up.

"Un uh. What you tryna hide?" Reign said and pulled her phone away. She turned her back to keep Unique from getting it back.

"Un uh! Chill!" she squealed as she tried to get it back. It was too little, too late when the onscreen Bryan kneeled behind her and slid inside of her with a 'Ssss!'.

"Yo! You fucked yo moms man?"

"No, he fucked me!" she said and shrugged her shoulders. Bryan didn't last long and slumped over on her back. "Barely."

"Wow!" Reign said, wide eyed. She handed the phone back and repeated, "Wow!"

"Wow is right and this nigga gonna need a second job cuz he gonna have to break me off!" she said indignantly. Bryan's dick had just gotten him in some trouble. Reign nodded in agreement since dude was foul for coming on to the girl. He was about to get what he had coming.

"Anyway, we going to the funeral?" Reign asked and held her breath.

Unique paused to think and thought it would look suspect if they didn't. The whole block always showed up to send off a fallen soldier, even if one of them made them fall. Many a funeral was attended by the person or persons who caused it.

"Yup. We going. I better go get dressed," she said and stood. She took one last toke from the blunt and headed out the door.

"Let me get fly," Reign said to herself and hoisted herself off the sofa. She headed into her closet to find something to wear to the funeral of the man she'd killed with the money she'd taken from him.

*****

"What you doing, ma?" Unique whined when she returned home to find her mother searching her room. It wasn't the first nor would it be the last time and there wasn't anything she could do about it. Complaints would be answered with reminders that she didn't pay the rent. 'This is my house' and other assorted blah, blah, blah that Unique wasn't trying to hear.

"You got weed?" Simone asked, explaining what she was looking for. That didn't explain the shirt and sneakers she'd pulled out of her closet and sat to the side.

"Yes, ma. Here!" she said, fighting to control her tone. Unlike Sharon, who tolerated Reign's mouth, Simone would fight her for mouthing off.

"Okay, thanks cuz Bryan damn tripping," she said with a hand out to accept the handout. Bryan had splurged on his date with Sharon and eating ass and didn't have any extra for her.

"And my sneakers?" she asked and pressed her lips tight to keep a smart aleck remark from seeping out.

"Oh yeah, let me rock this to work," she asked, minus the question mark.

Unique almost started a fight when she just waved her off. She had nothing to say until she left her room. "That's why I fucked your man," she teased under her breath. A second thought followed and she added, "And I'ma fuck him again."

"What you say, mama?" Simone called from the hallway, hearing a wisp of her daughter's voice.

"Nothing, ma. Just getting ready for this funeral!" she called back.

"Oh yeah!" Simone said, returning to her doorway. "That was crazy, yo! Don't nobody know what happened?"

"Nah," Unique said and she should know since she had her ear to the street. Speculation put it a few blocks up on 170th Street and that was fine with her.

"That young nigga was fine, too! He could have got it," Simone said, causing her daughter to grimace in disgust.

"Ma!" she spat back. Not because Tito wasn't fine but because she'd slept with him herself. She quickly remembered being bent over on her bed by her mother's man and shook it off. "Well, let me get dressed."

Unique did get dressed in new clothes and a new coat thanks to Tito's unwilling contribution. She laced her new boots tight and stepped out into the cold. The rest of the girls had gathered in front of Reign's building for the trek uptown to the cemetery.

Lisa made sure to lean over and honk the horn of the car she was riding in. Seven had cut her all the way off so she'd moved on to the next man.

"We shoulda took a cab," Reign grumbled under her breath as they walked over to the bus stop on Ogden Ave.

"Then we would have to explain to these broke bitches where we got carfare from," Unique sighed. She had the answer because she had asked herself the same question.

An hour and a half later, the crew arrived at Woodlawn Cemetery to pay their last respects. Both Reign and Unique looked in the direction of Reef's grave as the preacher preached. The tears running down their cheeks were real, just not for Tito. Both missed most of what was said but they weren't trying to hear it anyway. They were relieved when Tito was finally lowered into the ground.

"Y'all go 'head. I'm going to my brother's grave," Reign said and didn't wait for Neta and company to reply.

"Me too. See y'all back on the block," Unique said and rushed to catch up. It was a good walk over to Reef's final resting spot but he wasn't alone when they got there.

"Seven?" Reign asked curiously since she didn't see him at Tito's funeral.

"Yeah, I had to, um, holla at my man," he said, leaving out the part of not really fucking with Tito like that. He'd only tolerated him when he was the plug. Reef, he respected and came to show his respect.

"Me too!" Unique said and lifted her chin. She was still bragging about the man even though he was dead and buried.

"Okay, I'm out. Y'all need a ride back to the block?" he asked as he turned to leave.

"Yes," Reign said.

"No," Unique said at the same time.

Reign wasn't with whatever Unique had going on and spoke up for the both of them. "Yeah, we need a ride. Give us a few," she said while her friend pouted. A few minutes passed and he led them to a car.

"Yo, who car is this?" Unique demanded when the sedan responded to the key fob. It looked more like a family car than something a dope boy would be driving.

"My aunt's," he said since it was in her name. She didn't need to know that he made the payments so he kept it to himself. Cops didn't look twice at him in the plain Jane sedan but pulled over his counterparts in flashy whips with banging sound systems.

Reign twisted her lips at her friend when she moved on the front seat. For all her shade, it would seem like she would want to ride in the back. Reign didn't want to ride shotgun with his cute ass anyway so she didn't complain.

"You got weed?" Unique demanded with way more attitude than someone asking for something is supposed to have.

"Yeah but I'm not giving you none. You pregnant. You ain't supposed to be smoking," he shot back and braced himself.

"You ain't my daddy or my baby daddy!" Unique shot back. She read him the riot act most of the way home.

Reign listened with mixed emotions. The God-given maternal instinct told her smoking while pregnant was fucked up but everyone else was doing it. That was the reason she and most kids did things they shouldn't do. Some do things they don't even want to do but pressure can bust pipes and peer pressure can knock down a building. She often wondered how she ended up pregnant at 16 but everyone else was doing it.

"Thank God," Seven sighed when they reached the block.

Unique had yapped the whole way back home. She was still yapping as they got out of the car. "Un uh, don't be thanking God cuz God don't like ugly! I can't stand yo ugly butt!" she said as she unbuckled her seatbelt and stepped out. Seven could see her mouth moving in his rearview mirror as he drove away.

"Girl, you be giving him the business!" Reign said, shaking her head.

"I can't stand him," she giggled and followed her inside her building.

Sharon was on her way out as they came in.

"Where you going?" Reign demanded and Unique added, "Looking all cute!"

"Thank you, sweetie. Tell your buddy I don't answer to her," Sharon laughed. She was in a great mood and did look cute in tight jeans and a tight sweater. She was grown lady fine but the smile on her face lit up the day.

"Hmp," Reign huffed and walked away. Sharon got a giggle out of it and went on to meet her boyfriend.

She decided to cut to the chase and meet Bryan at the Motor Lodge. She could feed herself but she couldn't fuck herself. Sharon saw Bryan's car down the street and lifted her head high. She held her hand high as well and hailed a taxi. Since he was late, she went ahead and rented the room then texted him the room number.

"You up to something," Simone pursed her lips and nodding knowingly. She'd cheated enough to know one when she saw one. He had managed to juggle a side chick but two was cutting into her money. Add a third with Unique and his money was getting stretched thin. Unique was right; he was going to need a second job.

"Who?" he asked despite being the only other person in the room.

"You. Mmhm. You changing," she said, pointing at him so he couldn't ask 'who' again. She was right, too, because the quickest way to find out if a partner is cheating is them changing their routine. A person doesn't need pictures or proof. Doing things they didn't do before is proof enough.

"I don't know what you're talking about. I have to go home sometime. I have to work," he fussed.

"Mmhm, so let me give you some head before you go," she dared. She'd noticed that he'd been a lot less frisky lately. He didn't break her off last time he was over because he gave it to Unique. His money, too, and Simone was feeling the pinch.

"I don't have time," he declined. He really didn't since it was time to meet Sharon. Not to mention that they had exchanged dirty texts about oral sex over the last few days. She'd agreed to return the favor and he was eager to get to her.

"Mmhm," she repeated as he turned and left the room.

He bumped into Unique as she was coming in. It was the first time they'd seen each other since he ate her ass.

"Um, hey," Unique said nervously. She had to find the time and opportunity to drop the hammer on him. He was going to have to buy her silence and it wasn't going to be cheap.

"Hey yaself," he greeted almost flirtatiously. He looked down the hall to where her mother was and sighed. He was looking forward to catching her alone again. "I gotta run."

"Okay. See ya," she shrugged since she knew she would see him later. Her vagina gave a little throb and she couldn't wait to see him again.

Bryan whipped over the few blocks and pulled into the parking lot of the Motor Lodge. He looked up at the room numbers so he could park as close as possible. He parked next to a man leaned back in his seat with his eyes closed. A moment later, a woman popped her head up. Kidd's mother swung the door open and stepped out in front of Bryan and spit a mouthful of cum on the asphalt.

"Want yo dick sucked?" she asked, pointing at Bryan.

"I sure do," he laughed and headed up to the room. He had every intention of swinging downtown between Sharon's thick thighs and hoped she would, too.

Sharon let out a nervous sigh when she read the text announcing his arrival. She stood to look out the window but he was already knocking at the door. She sighed again and pulled it open wearing nothing but a naughty grin.

"Sorry I'm late, I... oh my!" he said and marveled at her body.

"Don't let the world see!" she said and pulled him inside. He immediately shoved his tongue into her mouth and grabbed two handfuls of ass. She pulled away and instructed, "Take off your clothes!"

Bryan backed up and stepped out of his clothing. His dick stood straight out when he reached his birthday suit. Sharon directed him onto his back on the bed and kissed his mouth, chin and Adam's apple. She twirled her tongue around his nipples before sucking each one.

"Mmm," Bryan moaned when her warm hand wrapped around his throbbing erection.

She stroked it firmly and stuck her tongue in his belly button. He moaned again when she rubbed his hard dick over her soft cheeks, lips and nose. It only got better when her lips parted slightly, allowing him to feel the heat and moisture of her mouth.

Sharon had only sucked two dicks in life but opened her mouth and made it a third. It wasn't as good when compared to Simone but his dick was in her mouth and that's all that mattered.

She actually had fun just like she did when she did her husband back in the day. He was one of the two and she would do him any time of day or night. Roscoe liked his dick sucked so she sucked it every chance she got. Why wouldn't she when he saved her? It was going well until it went wrong.

"Shit!" Bryan cursed and grabbed her head.

That reminded her of the other man who had been in her mouth. The nasty nigga her mother had brought home and called her husband. He would grip her head just like this and fuck her face. Bryan didn't notice she'd left the building as he humped her mouth. Meanwhile, she was transported back in time to a bad place.

*"Open, open!" her stepfather would demand while pressing his dick head against her lips and pressing her cheeks with his fingers. Once her mouth opened, he would shove himself inside and hold her head firmly.*

*"You choking her!" her mother complained from the sidelines. She wasn't worried so much about her husband putting his dick in her daughter's mouth, just not so far.*

*Sharon choked, causing tears to stream down her face.*

*"Mm, there, it...is!" he grunted and exploded in her mouth. She refused to swallow no matter what they said, so cum skeeted from the corners of her mouth and ran down her chin. "Shit!"*

*"Good girl, Sharon. Go get cleaned up so we can go out," her mother directed. "Oh, and happy birthday, baby...*

"Ugh!" Bryan grunted and let go.

Thirty-eight-year-old Sharon reverted back to sixteen and refused to swallow. She let him cum in her mouth and let it run back out. He was so excited that he missed the tears on her cheeks as he switched places with her.

The flashback was forgotten the second his tongue touched her slit. Her back arched off the bed when he clamped his lips over her vagina and sucked a nut out of her. They were even when she came in his mouth, too.

"Un un, put that on!" she insisted and pointed at the roll of rubbers she'd placed on the nightstand.

Bryan shrugged and rolled one down his shaft and shoved himself inside of her. She gladly sucked her own juices from his tongue, lips and chin while he got a good stroke going. It didn't take long for her lonely vagina to contract and cum all over his dick. She beat him by a few seconds before he grunted again and pumped the condom full of cum.

They went two more rounds before Sharon had to get home to get ready to go to work.

# Chapter 8

"Oh boy!" Unique said loudly and twisted her lips when she entered the bodega and saw Lisa at the counter buying a forty-ounce and a lighter.

Lisa snapped her head in her direction with a wicked snarl on her face. It changed into a wicked smile when she saw Unique and saw she was alone. She'd been waiting for an opportunity to catch her alone to ask about this rumor she'd heard.

"Yo, what's this I hear about this 'sposed to be Reef's baby?" she said, getting in her face and poking her rounded belly.

"And?" Unique shot back since she wasn't a punk, with or without her friends. Not much scared her but Lisa flipping a switchblade out and pointing at her belly scared the shit out of her.

"And bitch if you was fucking with MY baby father behind my back, I'ma cut your damn head off! Try me!" she said with menthol and malice on her breath.

Unique was the smart one and knew to keep her mouth shut.

"Hey, take that outside!" the clerk demanded from behind the counter.

"On God, if that's Reef's kid, I'ma kill you and it. That's my word," Lisa warned with an eerie calm. Her life was unraveling by the day and she was getting higher and higher to cope. She had slung her vagina far and wide like a fisherman's net but couldn't catch a baller. They would just hit it, quit it and forget it.

"Okay!" Unique whined but stopped short of denouncing her baby's father.

Lisa paused for a second to seriously contemplate taking her life right there, right then. "Let me find out. Swear on my child, I'ma..." she mumbled threats as she departed the store.

Unique stood frozen in place for several moments until the clerk spoke up again.

"You buying something or what?" he asked as if he had something else to do beside sell beer, baby formula and blunts.

"Uh, yeah, um, let me get two strawberry blunt wraps," she said, passing her money over the counter. Her cash was dwindling except what she'd put away from the Tito thing. That was for when the baby was born, if it lasted that long.

"Hmp!" the clerk huffed and made a big deal of looking down at her round belly. It didn't stop him from selling them to her or her from buying them. Her own mother was still smoking weed every day so the clerk wasn't talking about nothing.

*****

"Girl, what the hell is wrong with you?" Reign asked when she opened the door to let Unique in.

She had a faraway look in her eyes and was shaking like a leaf. She rushed inside as soon as the door opened. "Li, Li,Li, Lisa threa, threa, threatened to ki, kill me!" she managed to push past the lump of fear stuck in her throat. She cleared her throat but it was still there. She watched as Reign locked the multiple locks on the door so Lisa couldn't get in.

"What?" Reign shot back indignantly and began unlocking the locks she'd just locked. "Let's go beat that bitch ass!"

"No! She's crazy!" she said and leaned against the door to prevent her from opening it. She could still see the look of lunacy in Lisa's eyes. "She ha, had a kn, knife!"

"And I got a gu, gu, gun!" Reign spat and went to go get it. She returned a minute later with the same weapon used to kill Tito since she didn't have enough sense to get rid of the dirty gun.

"Reign, we can't just go shoot her down in the street!" Unique reasoned. Partly because it was unreasonable, but partly because she was scared.

"Well..." Reign said and sat because she knew her friend was right. She would have marched out and gunned the woman down in front of everyone out.

"Can you roll?" Unique asked but passed the wraps and weed before she nodded her head.

"She got to get hers, yo. Sick of that bitch!" she griped as she twisted up the last of the weed. Their tight faces began to relax with every toke from the blunt. By the end of the first one, they were both relaxed and happy.

"Girl, you seen them new Timbs? I got to have them!" Reign cheered. She too had vowed to save her Tito money for when her child was born. She knew Rankin would come drink more cum and break her off so she could afford to spend.

"Word. You seen the earrings Remy Ma had on in her new video? I'ma get me a pair made, too! Papi can make anything you bring him!" Unique added. They went back and forth until they decided to go shopping.

Unique rushed home to get her money so they could go up to Fordham Road. She scrunched her face up when she counted her money again. She'd had just over four thousand but now it was just under. She knew she'd chipped away at it from time to time but not that much. She shrugged and took it all.

"Where you going?" Simone asked when she ran into her in the hallway.

"Um, with Reign..." she replied, leaving out the 'where' because she would want to go. "We ain't doing nothing."

"Oh, okay. I gotta work anyway," Simone sighed.

"Where's Bryan?" Unique asked casually on the inside but buzzing on the inside. She was hoping he was coming over so she could kill two birds with one stone. The weed had her high and horny, plus she needed some money.

"I'on know, girl, he bugging lately. If I ain't know no better, I would swear he got another bitch somewhere," she replied, waving her hand like she didn't care even though she cared plenty.

"Oh, okay. I'm out," Unique said and turned to leave. She met up with Reign and tricked off almost all of her money. Her baby was going to need its own job because she couldn't handle money.

"Man, I spent way too much money," Reign said with her new earrings jingling as she shook her head. They were spending even more money, taking yet another cab all the way across their borough. "Guess I'ma have to get my pussy ate."

"Don't forget that nigga violated you!" Unique reminded hotly and wiped the smile off her friend's face.

"I'm not. He gone get his but he gotta pay first. He talking 'bout a spot for me and the baby. You know he gonna stash work at the crib. When he do, I'm gonna knock his blood clot ras clot ass off!" Reign vowed.

"Mmhm, don't lose focus, son," her bestie insisted. "Anyway, I gotta keep my shit at your spot. My moms be tripping, straight up robbing my ass!"

"My moms getting some dick now so she been chilling," Reign said with a tinge of jealousy since she wanted a boyfriend, too. They rode in silent thought until they reached the block and saw their crew outside. "Shit, and we got all this stuff."

"Bitches gonna be all in our business," Unique fussed even though pulling up in a taxi with new jewelry and thousands of dollars' worth of clothes and shoes broadcasted their business up and down the block.

"I know, right?" Reign agreed and paid the driver.

As expected, the flock of hood rats made a beeline over to them.

"Uh oh, someone balling!" Jewel cheered happily even though her heart felt envy. She didn't have anything so why would she want to see anyone else with something?

"Yeah, my moms broke bread," Reign explained since it would be more reasonable from her. Simone had just came out and asked who had some weed so they knew she had no bread to break.

"Smoke one then," Neta said, hoping to get something out of them.

"A'ight, let me put my stuff down," she said and led Unique upstairs.

"I don't even want to know," Sharon said when she saw the girls came in loaded down.

"Good," Reign huffed under her breath on the way down the hall. They put their bags down and took some weed out of their stash and headed back down.

*****

Reign was good and high when Rankin knocked on her door after conducting business with Seven. He licked his lips anxiously, ready to part with some of the money he'd just collected. Little did the dope boys know, they were working for Reign.

"Come in," Reign said as she opened the door. She was already turned on so she made sure not to look directly at him. She had a jiggle under her T-shirt since she didn't have panties on. They would have been wet from the anticipation already if she did.

"Lawda mercy!" he said, feeling his dick jump. He couldn't wait for her to have this baby so he could slide back inside her good, young poom-poom.

"I know, right!" she giggled and sat on the sofa. She kicked her thick thighs wide and dinner was served.

Rankin removed his dick from his pants as he took position between her legs. His twirling tongue coaxed a couple of nuts out of her before he stroked himself to one. Reign liked watching him cum and leaned up as he busted on her legs and stomach.

"Next week?" Rankin asked as he broke her off five hundred dollars.

"Mmhm," she agreed. She would have agreed if he said tomorrow too since he was paying. She locked the door behind him and went to wash his nut off.

Rankin exited the building and walked towards his car.

"Hey, stupid," Lisa called out with a drunken giggle. Rankin looked around to see who she could have meant even though she was looking right at him. "Yeah, you dummy!"

"Whata gwan?" he asked, cocking his head. She had been flirty with him too but he never took the bait. Now she was being downright disrespectful and he had no qualms about beating a bitch up. He frowned up as she approached with some news.

"She playing you, you know? Got you thinking that's your baby but she fucked the whole block," Lisa lied and cackled like the wicked witch of the west side.

Rankin squinted since it helped him think better and thought. He had no proof Reign was growing his seed except his guilt over taking the pussy in a drunken rage. There was the blood, but she'd also offered to sell him some pussy before he got his head busted. He'd just parted with half a grand and all he had to show for it was dried pussy juice in his beard.

"Mmhm, nigga," she laughed, seeing the wheels turning in his head. "Come on up and get yo dick sucked."

The dread had just jacked off on Reign's leg while he ate her out but still accepted the blow job. He followed inside her building and up to her apartment.

"Let me get the room," Lisa barked at her mother as she led the dread inside.

She let out a sigh that said what she thought of her new daughter and retreated to her room. Lisa had Rankin in her mouth before her mother sat on her bed.

"Ras clot," the Jamaican cursed in a mix of confusion and pleasure. Again he wondered if Reign was playing him but Lisa sure was sucking that dick.

She sucked his large, mushroom shaped head while tugging the thick shaft. She used her free hand to shimmy out of her jeans. "Mmm," Lisa moaned when he reached down and fondled her sopping wet box. "Come on."

Rankin didn't need to be told twice to get some pussy. He fell on top of her and shoved himself inside. The nut he'd just busted on Reign's leg had just warmed up his engine and he commenced to beat the pussy up. Lisa knew this was her shot at bagging the man and pulled out all the stops. She pulled her legs up and let him pound on her cervix.

"Blood clot!" he shouted as the end drew near.

"Let me get it! Aaaah," she said and opened wide. Her tonsils dangled like a target and gave him something to shoot for. He pulled out and rushed into her mouth to unload.

"Lawda mercy!" he repeated as he skeeted down her throat.

She worked his balls with her hand and swallowed in loud, dramatic gulps.

Rankin thanked her with a bag of personal weed from his pocket and headed out the door. He had a lot to think about so he went home to think.

*****

Unique had to wait another week until she and Bryan were alone again. They shared conspiratorial glances while Simone prepared for work. He pretended to get sleepy just before it was time for her to leave so he wouldn't have to drive her.

"Yo, hold it down so my man can sleep," she advised as she passed through the living room

"Kay," Unique complied and turned the TV down a few notches. She hopped up into the window to watch her mother leave the block like Reign always did but for different reasons. Reign waited for her mother to leave so she could smoke weed in the house. Unique watched her mother leave so she could fuck her man.

"Mmm," Bryan moaned as he came up behind Unique and gripped her butt cheeks. She moaned with him when he leaned in and kissed her neck.

"Sss," she hissed when he stuck his hand down the front of her panties and played in her pussy.

He spun her around on the sofa and stuck his tongue down her throat. He was already butt naked except for a raging erection. Unique gripped it and fondled it as their tongues thrashed in each other's mouths.

"Eat it," she pleaded and lay back. Bryan couldn't wait to eat her and fell between her legs to comply. He pushed her legs wide and tongue lashed her clit and anus until she came with a violent shudder.

"My turn?" he asked and moved his dick towards her face. She allowed him to rub it on her lips but never opened up. He needed to be inside of her so he positioned her halfway off the sofa so he could fuck her without putting his weight on the baby in her belly.

"Oww," she fussed and grimaced as he worked himself inside. Once he was in, he took slow, easy strokes. Not many though because that tight, young girl pussy got the best of him again. Once again, he pushed in deeply and came inside of her.

"Shit!!!" He shivered and shook as he exploded in her. He stayed in and stayed hard for round two. Round two lasted just a few strokes longer than the first.

"Let me see," Unique requested and leaned up to watch him cum on her stomach. They kissed again as if they were the couple and not he and her mom. Once he went soft, she went hard and stated her case.

"Yo, you gotta pay me for this. And to keep quiet. You not gonna be fucking me for free anytime you feel like it."

"Of course! I always have a few dollars for you!" he shot back. He shorted his wife this time so he could afford to break off both the mother and daughter. He rushed to Simone's room and came back with a hundred bucks.

"You gotta do better than that!" she said as she took the money. Reign had gotten a thousand dollars from Rankin and she figured her pussy was just as valuable. "I need a thousand dollars."

"I'm not giving you a thousand dollars!" Bryan chuckled like it was ludicrous. His laughter insulted her but she had a comeback of her own.

"You will if you don't want my moms to see this..." Unique said and reached for her phone. The video of him eating her ass wiped the smile off his face just like a warm, soapy wash rag wipes away dirt. "Not to mention child protective services. I'm pretty sure I'm too young to have my ass ate by a grown man."

"Or..." he said and snatched the phone away. She pursed her lips sarcastically while he scrambled to remove the SD card. He caught her expression and caught on immediately. "You have another copy, huh?"

"I have several copies," she laughed even though she didn't find it funny. He played her mother by coming on to her and now he was trying to play her. "Now I'ma need another five hundred for my baby."

"Your mother is going to be madder at you than me!" he pleaded. He tried several angles to change her mind and stop her head from shaking but nothing worked.

"Fifteen hundred," she insisted and didn't budge. She extended her hand for her money.

"Well, I don't have it on me now!" he said and raised his hands to show he was still naked. "I'll get it and bring it back. Shoot, for fifteen hundred I should at least get some head."

"You should, but not from me," Unique giggled.

"Well, I want some more pussy then," he demanded and got it. Unique laid back and spread her legs for him.

Bryan rubbed his soft dick against her soft lips until it was hard and they were wet. It was the perfect combination and he pushed back inside of her. This time he fucked her with a grudge and beat the pussy up.

# Chapter 9

"So what we gonna do? We gotta do something for our 17th birthdays!" Reign said since their birthdays were two days apart and two days away.

"I'on know. Bryan was supposed to bring me my money two days ago," Unique pouted. Not only had he not come back to pay her, he hadn't come back at all.

"Hmp," Reign added since Rankin hadn't come by to make her cum over the weekend. She saw him when he came on the block and got ready to get eaten but he never came upstairs. Not her stairs, anyway, since Lisa fucked and sucked him so good last time that he went back for seconds.

Both girls were close to broke since they couldn't stop shopping. They had a ton of new clothes and sneakers waiting for them to give birth and lose weight so they could be worn, though.

"We can't do much anyway with these babies in us," Unique said, placing a hand on her stomach as her baby moved inside. Last year, they'd hit the skating rink for their birthdays. They drank, smoked and turned up until dawn. Now they both weaned off the weed as they entered their third trimesters.

"Well, we can asked my moms to cook and get our eat on!" her friend suggested. A good portion of their money went straight into their mouths. "Ooh, we can get us some crab legs! And chicken, and macaroni..."

"I want fish and spaghetti and..." Reign added and added her own two cents on the birthday menu.

"What you two talking about?" Sharon asked as she came out of her room. Her cute outfit said she wasn't going to work and the pleasant smile said she was about to get laid.

"Our birthday meal! Can you cook for us? Please!" Unique pleaded.

"Sure. Let me know what you guys want and I'll hook it up," she said and retrieved her coat from the closet.

"Where you going, ma?" Reign asked even though it was obvious since she was all cute.

"To see my friend," Sharon said with a sly smile since she was about to get laid. She, like every woman, would love to be wined and dined, and to ride carriage through Central Park even but she settled for some dick. Dick is better than no dick so she fed herself and went to get laid.

"Yo' moms getting to it!" Unique cheered. She was getting some, too, so she was happy for her.

"Yeah," Reign sighed a lonely sigh. She actually missed Rankin's big tongue almost as much as his money.

Sharon met Bryan at the same motel and tried new positions and ended up with the same results. She curled up into his arms and began to go to sleep. As much as Bryan would have loved to let her so they could wake up and fuck again, he couldn't. He had just hit his 401k for a little cash to keep Unique quiet. Not to mention that he wanted to fuck her again. Sure, he would pay the ransom but she was going to take some dick with it.

"Baby, I have to go," he said, gently shaking Sharon back awake.

"What, to see your other woman?" she asked and twisted her lips. Even if a woman comes in knowing she's a side piece, she going to want to be the main entree eventually. Especially when she thought she was better than the first chick. Sharon thought that with their combined salaries they could get a house on Long Island and live well. She was right, too, because that's exactly what Bryan and his wife were doing now. He just kept a few chicks on the side.

"Yeah..." he sighed, true to the burden Simone had become. Knocking her up was just the dumbest shit in the world. She'd told him she was on the pill but didn't say what kind. He pumped her full of cum until she came up pregnant. The bright side was Unique. Her good, young pussy was worth every cent he had to give her. He withdrew a grand for her and another one for her mother.

"You need to upgrade. Slumming with Simone instead of shining with Sharon," Sharon suggested and struck a pose in her bra and panties.

"Yeah," he replied and sighed again. His own wife used to look like that a couple hundred pounds ago. She was a bad little thing before the kids. Have him tell it, that's why he creeps.

"Well, it's out there now. All you have to do is grab it," she said and shrugged. The show ended when she shimmied back into her jeans and pulled her sweater back over her head.

"Let me give you a ride," Bryan offered instead of letting her catch a cab. It was the least he could do after the way she just rode him backwards.

"Nah, I'm good," she declined and stepped from the room. A taxi had just emptied its horny passengers at the office so she jumped in.

Bryan dressed and followed over to 164th in his own car. "Here we go," he groaned as he parked in front of Simone's building and got out. He entered and hopped up the stairs to her apartment.

"Neek! Get the door! Neek! Shit!" she fussed when she remembered Unique went to spend the night with Reign. She had no choice but to roll out of bed and see who was knocking. She checked her phone and saw Bryan still hadn't returned her calls or texts so she was shocked to see him when she opened the door. "Mmhm."

"A lot going on," he said as she turned around and walked away. He glanced over to the sofa for Unique but it was empty. He watched her large ass shift as he followed her to the room. He wondered if he had one more in him after the tryst with Sharon.

"Mmhm," she repeated and twisted her lips as she entered her room and plopped on her bed.

"Yeah, well, here," he said and handed her some money.

That untwisted her lips into a smile. "Thank you, daddy! You want some head?" she asked, ready to roll down and give him some. As many free dicks as she'd sucked in her life, she would definitely suck one for a grand.

"I'm good. Just wanna get some sleep," he said and stretched out. "Where's Unique?"

"Sleep over at her friends," she answered instead of asking why he was asking about her when she'd asked about getting his dick sucked. Not that he would have told her, but his plan to have her do it.

Bryan nodded and blinked until he began to snore. Simone made sure he was asleep before digging his phone out. She looked at the trail his finger left and used it to unlock the phone. Luckily for him, his wife did the same so he cleaned up behind himself most of the time.

He kept some porn in the video gallery but so did she and most people she knew. She watched some young girl give some grown man head for a minute then turned it off and cuddled up against her man and went to sleep.

*****

"Ooh, ooh! Bryan here! He better have my money!" Unique sang when she saw Bryan's car from Reign's window.

"You stupid!" Reign laughed as her friend scrambled to get dressed. "Get that money, girl!"

"Oh, and I plan to!" she said and rushed from the apartment. Her eyes lit up when she saw Seven step from his building then narrowed into jealous slits when a young girl stepped out behind him.

Seven was enjoying being king for a day and all that came with it. Mostly the money which was stacking up faster than he could have dreamed. Then there was the ton of pussy that came along with the job. He'd gotten plenty just for being a pretty boy but now it was ridiculous.

"Sup, Unique?" he greeted like he always did.

She replied like she always did and turned her nose up at him. She wanted to twist her hips as she walked away but being pregnant stood in her way. "Hmp!" she huffed, tilted her head high and marched into her own building.

Her mother and Bryan were in the middle of a discussion when she walked in.

"But I don't feel like going in!" Simone whined. It was time for her to go to work but the thousand dollars she'd gotten for free made her want to stay home.

"That has to last you. Money is...tight," he said as Unique walked in. He knew money made her lethargic and that he should have spoon-fed it to her.

"Hey, lil mama. I got something for you," Simone told her daughter when she walked in.

"Okay. Hey, Mr Bryan," she said and waddled down to her room.

Her mother came in behind her and dug into her pocket. "Here, baby," she said and broke her off a hundred dollars.

"What's this for, ma?" she asked as she accepted the money.

"For my grandbaby. Don't blow it on weed and food!" she insisted even though she planned to.

"I'on even smoke no more!" she said but didn't say anything about food. In fact, she was thinking about what she was going to eat next. It wasn't what she thought it would be, though.

"Well, I gotta go to work. Bryan probably gone chill till he go to work," she said and left her alone.

Unique immediately changed into her around the house uniform of T-shirt and panties, except without the panties.

"I still think you could drive me," Simone said and twisted her lips at what she knew was coming.

"I just gave you money. Take a cab, let me get some sleep before I go to work," he repeated.

"Oh okay," she sighed and prepared to leave. Her job was generous enough to provide a stool so she could sit at her register for eight hours. That gave Bryan at least four hours to spend with her daughter before he went to work herself.

Both Bryan and Unique watched from the window as Simone hailed and caught a taxi. They waited until it bent the corner and came out the bedrooms at the same time.

"Hey," Unique giggled when she saw they were on the same page. She also saw the lump in his around the house sweatpants.

"Hey yourself," he said and followed her wide ass into the living room. He had cash in one hand and his phone in the other.

There was an awkward moment of silence when they reached the sofa until Unique saw green in his hand. "Is that my money?" she asked, trying to sound hard since it was extortion and all. That didn't stop her pussy from getting wet from anticipation.

"Yup but..." he agreed and paused so she would ask...

"But what?" she asked to see what stood in the way of her getting her money.

"You gotta do something for me too, though," he said and finished the thought by removing his dick. It was hard from that same anticipation. He wanted his dick sucked but couldn't wait to get back inside of her.

"Mmhm," she said, twisting her lips as she reached out and took it in her hand. She gave it a few strokes before leaning in and kissing its big head. "I never...done...this...be...fore."

"Mm, put it in your mouth," he directed, literally since he'd begun to record. Unique looked up at the phone with a mouthful of dick and fluttered her eyes. "That's it..."

Bryan watched through his screen as Unique gave the second blowjob of her life. It wouldn't be her last because she enjoyed doing it and his reaction. His legs rocked and he moaned and breathed heavily. All signs she recalled from the last time she'd sucked dick on camera on this same sofa. She pulled him out her mouth in the nick of time and watched him bust a nut on her shirt and his pants.

"Shit! I can't tell you never did it before!" he said and handed over the cash. That freed a hand to play in her pussy.

"Eat it," she ordered and he ate it. He too could tell when she was about to cum but unlike her, he didn't run. Instead, he clamped down and sucked all that good pussy juice down his throat.

"Been...waiting on...this!" he admitted as he worked his dick inside her.

"Me too," Unique heard herself grunt with pain and pleasure once he got his smooth stroke going. He usually took it easy on her but he'd just paid her a thousand dollars, his fee to fuck the shit out of her, and that's exactly what he did.

Bryan pushed Unique's thick legs as far as they would go and pushed inside as far he could. He lifted her legs by her ankles and pounded his frustration away. She loved it and howled in delight and distress. Lucky for Unique she was young with a nearly new vagina and he couldn't hang.

"Good ass pussy!" he complained as he took a few final thrusts and busted inside of her.

"Mmhm," she said, knowing why he'd tried to punish her.

They both knew that once she spent the money she would be back for more. And he would pay her because he liked putting his dick in her. Not enough to pay her a thousand dollars each time but he was going to give her an allowance. Even if he had to pick up extra shifts.

"Yup," he laughed and stopped the recording. "I can't wait til you have that baby! I'ma take you to away for the weekend."

"My moms, too?" Unique asked and twisted her lips. Not that she wouldn't go but wanted to know how he planned to pull it off.

"Yeah, well..." was all he had at the moment. She would be his pick out of all the women in his life. Now he just had to figure out how to do it.

*****

"Mmhm," Bryan's wife Paula hummed and shook her head when her wayward husband found his way home. She put up with his philandering because he was still a good provider.

"What now?" he asked in exasperation, as if she was the one who barely slept in their own bed. He figured that was probably it and knew he may have to fuck her. It was a chore after she gained weight since his 'for better or worse' didn't include weight gain.

"The 401k. You already cut your daughter's allowance off and all extras for this family. Now you digging into our future? Robin's college? Our retirement?"

*She just want some dick*, Bryan thought to himself as she went on and on about what he was and wasn't doing.

Paula was a big, pretty woman when he met her but didn't shed her baby weight after giving birth. She gained more and he lost more desire for her. He accidentally cheated with another nurse and got away with it. He'd been cheating ever since.

"And then..." Paula said as he ignored her and undressed. She forgot what she was saying when his dick swung free as he stepped out of his drawers.

"You not taking your clothes off?" he asked and climbed on their bed.

"This doesn't change the fact that you're wasting our money," she fussed as she undressed.

Bryan turned away since she didn't look like the other women in his life. He reached under the covers and pulled on his dick while thinking of Unique. He thought about taking his phone into the bathroom to watch the video so he could get hard but it wasn't on the nightstand where he always kept it. In fact, it was on Simone's nightstand where he'd left it.

Paula's lonely vagina throbbed and flooded as she slid under the covers with her husband. He may not have remembered the last time he'd made love to her but she did. When he rolled on top of her and slid inside, it ended a six month, one week and three day dick drought.

"Damn," Bryan fussed curiously as he struggled to get inside his wife. He frowned up, wondering if she had always been this tight. "And wet!"

"Yeah, it is," Paula bragged and gave a Kegel squeeze to remind him what he was missing. Remind him that big, beautiful women got that good-good, wet-wet.

It was so good that he had to stick his tongue in her mouth like old times. They kissed as they alternated between making love and fucking during the same session. Bryan was out of bounds busting in Unique and her mother but had every right to cum in his wife.

"Shit! I'm...about to...cum!" he warned as he reached the point of no return.

"Cum, baby," she urged and rubbed his back.

"Okay, baby, here, I, cu... Ugh! Shit! Mm," he grunted and filled her up.

Filled her up at the exact second Simone opened his phone back in the Bronx.

# Chapter 10

"See what you got me doing? See what you missing since you...ain't...here?" Simone narrated as she pointed his phone at her pussy while playing in it. The high-end phone perfectly showed the glistening wetness on her fingers as well as the squishing sounds of her soaked vagina.

He would definitely see it all when she shook and came all over her fingers. Couldn't miss all the creamy goodness coating her hand. It got so good that she doubled up and went for seconds. The second one ended like the first and she had a puddle under her pussy on the bed.

"Mmm, just for you. I love you," Simone said, and meant it, into the lens. She blew him a kiss and stopped the recording.

Feeling naughty, she decided to watch it again and went into the gallery. Ironically, she never found anything when she broke into his phone to search but now that she wasn't, she found it at.

"What the hell is this?" she frowned curiously when she saw her daughter with his dick in her mouth. She was so shook up that she cut it off and put the phone down to pretend she didn't see what she just saw. She picked it back up and started it from the top.

"I never...done...this...be...fore," the Unique on screen lied and put her mouth on him.

Tears burned as eyes as she watched her child suck her man off. It was plenty bad but got worse when he returned the favor and ate Unique to a screeching orgasm.

"Man, this some real bullshit," she wailed and tried to knock her tears away. It was futile because the tears just kept coming. To make matters worse, he didn't even eat her anymore.

Now she saw why. Sorrow turned to anger and anger turned to rage as Simone stood up to act.

\*\*\*\*\*

"You really ain't gonna hit this?" Neta asked and twisted her lips as a dare.

"Nope. Not until after I have my baby," Unique said, causing Reign to nod along in agreement.

"My sister smoked her whole pregnancy!" Jewel proclaimed and took a pull as they made their way home from school. Neta had sparked the weed the second they got off the bus. "She said it make the baby smaller!"

"Um..." Reign frowned. She couldn't find the words but somehow that just didn't sound good.

"I know I can't wait to have this baby," Unique said as they turned on to the block. She opened her mouth to say more but got confused when a crackhead scurried by wearing what looked like her jacket. She tried to dismiss it until she saw a pair of her sneakers on her feet and another pair in her hand. "Huh?"

"I thought I was bugging, yo," Reign said when she saw another junkie wearing some of Unique's clothing. They both saw why when they spotted a pack of addicts picking through a dwindling pile of clothing, shoes and personal effects.

"What the hell are you doing?" Unique shouted when her mother came out and added more of her belongings to the pile while her friends tried to stop the zombies from running off with her clothing.

"What am I doing? What am *I* doing?" Simone asked and inched closer.

Unique knew her mother well enough to duck when she swung on her. She dipped one blow and blocked two more. No one expected the kick to the belly that followed so it got through.

"Yo, Simone, you bugging!" a lady called out as Unique stumbled away.

"I'm bugging? This bitch fucking my man and I'm bugging? Shit, she probably pregnant by him!" she shrieked, sending the onlookers into shock. All heads turned in Unique's direction.

"This Reef baby in me!" Unique shot back indignantly. She was sorry until that wild allegation. "Oh, and I wasn't fucking your man, he was fucking me! Oh, and eating my ass!"

"Bitch, I'll kill yo lil ass!" Simone growled and tried to get at her.

Lucky for all, she was held back by the few people that didn't want to see the pregnant mother and daughter fighting in the middle of the street. They pulled their phones out for nothing because there was nothing to record.

The crew collected what was left and took it up to Reign's apartment since everyone knew that's where she was going.

"Don't bring yo fast ass back to my house!" her mother threatened as she was pulled back into her building.

"That's the State of New York's apartment. They the one pay the rent!" Unique shouted back. She was lucky to get a third of her belongings since her mother kept a third and the crackheads ran off with a third. Luckily, she'd kept most of her clothes at Reign's. Unluckily, her money was hidden in her room and she wasn't getting back in there anytime soon.

"What in the world is going on out there?" Sharon demanded when the pack of girls came into her apartment with armfuls of clothing. She had heard the commotion downstairs but didn't look out her window. There was always something going on and she would have to live in the window to catch it all.

"Simone just jumped on Unique!" Neta blurted so she could be first to spread the news.

"Said she pregnant by her man!" Jewel tossed in so she could get in on the gossip.

Sharon almost got whiplash from snapping her head in Unique's direction.

"Nuh uh! I'm pregnant by your son! My moms is crazy! Damn crackhead!" she shot back so fiercely that Sharon believed her.

"Okay, watch your mouth about your mother," Sharon warned, mainly for Reign's benefit. "No matter what you think of her, she's still your mother."

Unique pressed her lips together so she wouldn't say anything else. She didn't have to because the rest of the girls went in about what they thought of the woman. Sharon missed most of it thinking about Bryan. Simone was wild but would she just make this up? She had a date with him tomorrow night so she had to get to the bottom of this. That meant she had to go see Simone.

"You my mother," Unique moaned and went in for a hug. She and Sharon melted into each other and knew she was here to stay.

"Well, I still need to talk to your mother," she informed then cleared her house of hood rats. "Thanks, girls. Reign will be down after her homework is done."

"Okay!" Neta and the girls sang and went downstairs.

Sharon went to put a coat on so she could go speak with Simone.

"Man, that bitch got my money," Unique moaned. She'd put eight hundred dollars away from Bryan and had the change in her pocket.

"She gonna find it?" Reign asked, wide-eyed.

"Nah, I hid it in her room since she stay searching mine all the time," she said, finally getting a smile. Now all she had to do was wait until her mother went to work since she still had her keys.

*****

"Who?" Simone barked at the door when she heard a knock from the other side. She knew her daughter didn't have the balls to come back but she still snatched it open aggressively. "Oh. Hey, girl."

"What's going on? They say you put your daughter out?" Sharon asked and braced herself hoping not to hear what she heard. Simone stepped aside for her to enter so she did.

"Girl, I found out that little bitch was fucking my man," she said as if talking about some chick off the street, not from her womb.

"Unique? Are you sure? I wouldn't believe anything I heard off the streets. You how 'they said' and 'they heard' can be..." Sharon said, making excuses while Simone pulled up the video on Bryan's phone. She let the video speak for her when she turned it to Sharon.

"That's his dick in her mouth," Simone narrated unnecessarily since Sharon could identify both. She'd raised Unique so she could recognize her even with her face distorted from being stuffed with a dick. She saw Bryan's pretty dick in her dreams so she knew it was him even before she heard his voice.

"Mm, suck that dick," he said as he stroked her face.

"Wow," Sharon moaned in shock and disgust at seeing the teen girl with a grown man in her mouth. She knew she and Reign were obviously having sex but assumed with other teens like themselves. Even Reef wasn't much older than them but Bryan was her age. She'd had enough when Bryan came on her chest.

"Wow is right! I can't believe that little bitch! After all I do for her and she..." Simone ranted.

Sharon twisted her lips dubiously when the woman never mentioned Bryan in her rage. "So, what he saying?" she wanted to know. Purely out of curiosity because what was there to say? He'd fucked her daughter; that much was clear.

"Girl, he called asking if he left his phone here. I told him to come get it," she replied.

"And? Oh, you gone check his ass when he get here, huh?" Sharon asked. She was disgusted with him and wouldn't see him again but wasn't so sure about Simone.

"Huh? Oh, yeah. I'ma let him have it!" she said quite unconvincingly.

Sharon wished she could stay but had an extra shift and needed the extra money. Simone needed money, too, and the only 'it' she was going to let Bryan have was that plump, pregnant pussy between her legs.

*****

"There he go," Reign said when she saw Bryan pull onto the block. She had just took over the window to watch for him after Unique's shift ended. Unique rushed over and watched him park in front of her mother's building.

"Let me go around the corner so I can catch him when he leave," she said and put her coat on. She just knew Simone was going to snap on him too and throw him out. He would have to go down to the end of the block to get back to the expressway so that's where she would catch him.

He entered the building just as she exited Reign's.

"It's open!" Simone called out when he knocked on the door. He twisted the knob and walked in on her seated on the sofa. "Pull your dick out."

"Excuse me?" he chuckled as he didn't comprehend but complied.

"Now come here," she ordered and sat up straight. As soon as he was close enough, she leaned forward and took him into her mouth.

Bryan was greedy enough to look down the hall towards Unique's room, hoping to get in her mouth next. Simone grabbed his attention again when she gagged on his dick. She was either trying to please him or commit suicide by choking to death.

"Shit!" he said as the good head got better. She twisted her head sideways and worked her neck like she was thirsty and needed a drink. She got one a few strokes later when he grunted and skeeted in her mouth.

"Mmhm," she said and nodded in agreement with the torrent of cum coming out his dick. She greedily swallowed it down as fast as it exploded out. He wiggled and writhed in pleasure while his knees bucked and buckled but she wouldn't let him go. "You like that?"

"Hell yeah!" he cheered since she'd just scored a touchdown, home-run and hole in one.

"Good, so you don't have to fuck my daughter again then. Right?" she asked, reaching between her legs to get ready for round two.

"Huh?" he asked just like she expected so she answered by passing his phone to him with the video playing. His knees buckled when he flinched to make a run for it. Except Simone grabbed his dick to make sure he couldn't.

"Nuh uh, nigga, you ain't going nowhere! I know her fast ass came after you. Little bitch want everything I get!" she said even though everything she had on at the moment was pilfered from Unique's room when she kicked her out.

"I, um..." he started then stopped to let her lead them wherever they were going.

Inside her for now since she pulled him down and guided him inside her. Unique was standing at the end of the block while Bryan dug her mother out real good. In the end, he was forgiven since she wanted a man more than a child. Ironic since she had a child in her belly now to keep the man.

"What he say?" Reign asked when Unique returned an hour later.

"He never came. His car still at my moms?" she asked since she couldn't figure out why.

"Oh, wow!" she replied since she knew. "Yo, your moms mad at you but still fucking with dude. That's some real grimy shit!"

"And he the one started it!" Unique moaned and pouted like the kid she really was. She may have been hurt but Reign was fuming. It still didn't sit well with her that grown men pursued these kids. If it wasn't for Rankin coming after her, all this wouldn't be happening now.

"And we gone end it! Where that nigga stay?" she said with the wicked wheels turning in her head.

"I'on know. I heard him say something about Long Island," she recalled. The look on her friends face made her ask, "Why? What you gone do?"

"He not getting away with what he did. I'ma do something. I know that!" she vowed. She was plotting but she wasn't the only one on the block plotting.

***

"Sup Mike-Mike?" Seven greeted when he let him in to re-up.

"Chillin, just chillin," he said, looking all around. He saw the girl on the sofa and nodded.

"What you tryna cop?" he asked to hurry him along so he could get back to the girl on the sofa.

"Look-it. I'ma need the same thing but I'ma need you to front me a few, too, cuz I got some dudes from, um, Jersey, Long Island who, um, yeah," Mike-Mike said real fast.

"Nah. No credit for you, yo," he said since it wasn't fast enough. He wasn't sure how it would go so he sent his friend to his room, "Go to the back, yo."

Oh yeah! My bad. So I'll just come back and get that. Gotta get my other dough from, un, huh," he stammered.

Seven didn't see the envious glint in his eyes as he served him. Even if he did, he was too naïve to understand it. If he did, he would have gunned him down on the spot.

# Chapter 11

"Happy birthday, girls," Sharon sang as she served the girls their birthday meal. She'd splurged a little and sprang for lobster tails, crab legs and shrimp.

"Ooh, we balling!" Reign cheered when she saw the same foods the rappers rapped about on her plate.

"Thanks, ma!" Unique said and stood to hug her neck and kiss her cheek.

"You're welcome, girls. I wish I could join you but I have to work," she said even though she wasn't dressed for work. She was going but had a meeting before she went.

"Okay, ma," Reign said since she had some plans of her own. She needed some money before she spent the rest of what she had.

At the moment, the seafood spread took priority and they dug in. The only sounds to be heard were shells cracking and lips smacking.

"Hope you have better luck than me," Unique said and sighed. She still hadn't been able to get into her apartment to retrieve her money. Simone wasn't going back to work on a regular until she'd depleted the money Bryan had given her. She smoked and ate while watching TV all day.

"I hope I don't play myself like you did," she snickered back. She got a good kick out of her waiting down the block for Bryan while he was digging her mother out.

"Ha ha," she said and twisted her lips up. Only for a moment, though, before she cracked up, too. "Lucky is wasn't too cold!"

"Word," Reign said, glad it wasn't too cold tonight either since she planned to wait outside and catch Rankin when he came to supply the block and pick up his money. She wanted her pussy eaten almost as bad as she wanted some money.

They made small talk as Sharon made her way over to the motel she and Bryan always met at. She had her uniform in her bag so she could go to work for her shift. She twisted her lips up at his car she rarely got to ride in. Pride tilted her chin high and she marched on.

"Hello there," Bryan said in that deep baritone that sounded so good in her ear when he was deep inside of her. He'd taken a page from her book since he'd arrived first and wore nothing but a smile.

"Hello yourself," she said stoically as planned but couldn't help a downward glance at the meat dangling below. She caught herself and lifted her head again and marched in.

"Uh oh, spending the night with me?" he asked, seeing her bag. He immediately began to think of excuses to tell his wife since he'd promised to come home tonight.

"Nope," she quipped without explaining further and began to remove her pants and panties. She climb on the bed and asked, "Would you mind?"

"I wouldn't mind at all!" he said and dove between her thighs. He kissed the inside of her thighs and all around her vagina.

Sharon usually enjoyed the teasing but didn't have time for it tonight. She reached down and pulled his face into her pussy. "Sss, mmm," she hissed and moaned when he went straight to her sweet spot. It was sweet to him too and he lovingly lapped it up.

Sharon tried to hold off the impending explosion but that only made it worse. She had hoped to drag it out and make it last but it didn't work out that way when her legs began to shake. Bryan knew he had her and zoomed in. He prepared himself for the gush of juice she emitted when she came. She came and filled his mouth.

"Let...me get...this dick...in you!" he said urgently as he rose up her body to insert himself. She loved when he would plunge inside of her just after she came. Another nut was right around the corner whenever he did.

Not tonight, though, because she had other plans.

"Wait, hold up," she said, stopping him from entering her with her hand. "Get up for a second."

Bryan complied and put a confused look on his face when she rolled of the bed and stood. He squinted when she bent over to retrieve her panties and put them back on. Her pants were next and he finally asked, "What you doing?"

"Getting dressed. I have to work," she replied simply. She was waiting for him to ask why so she could explain.

"But... why?" he stammered as his erection deflated sadly.

"Why? because you had sex with a child. A sixteen-year-old child!" she shot back. She really wanted to fight him at the moment.

"Which child?" he asked, not realizing he was telling on himself. He liked young girls and would take them when he could find one.

"Which one?! Shit, how many you fucked?" she asked in shock. She was really shocked by the dumbfounded look on his face as if trying to count how many in his mind. "You know what? Unique, nigga. Simone's daughter! She may not care but I do! I have a daughter that age, too!"

"Reign, with her fine little ass!" he said, licking his lips. He'd accepted it was over and decided to chump her off. Mainly because he didn't know she was Roscoe's ex-wife and had no idea what she was capable of. He got a little taste when she popped him in his mouth.

"Bit..." he started to say and buck back but saw the look in her eyes. The hollow look of a killer before they kill and backed off. He raised his hands in surrender and backed away.

"Thought so," she shot like a tough girl and finished dressing.

She stormed out the room, leaving the door wide open and marched away.

*****

Mike-Mike watched and plotted all week and figured that Seven should have plenty of bread on a Saturday night.

He was right, too, since that was the night he would pay Rankin what he was owed and re-up. He was going through so much coke that he had to meet with Tariq's partner Quan every couple days. The coke business boomed beyond what he'd imagined. He was able to stack a hundred grand in no time. It was his target goal to quit and move down south. It came so quickly that he decided to make it two hundred, then quit and move down south. The prisons and graveyards are full of dudes who were after one last score.

He built his nerve up and marched towards Seven's building but Rankin pulled a loud Buju Banton blaring stop and got out. He had a duffle bag full of weed with him when he went into the building. He thought about catching him on the stairs but didn't want those problems. Seven was a softer target so he waited.

"Rude mon!" Seven greeted when he pulled the door open with a smile.

"Whata gwan, yout?" he smiled back because he liked the kid. He reminded him so much of Reef when they'd first started doing business.

"Chillin," he said and led him to the sofa. Neat stacks of money adorned the coffee table as an offering. "Need to count it?"

"No, mon. You good money," he said and began removing the weed from the bag. "You need ta put 'pon da scale?"

"Nah, you good money, too!" he laughed.

Rankin pulled a baggie of buds that looked more like fruity pebbles than weed.

"Well damn!" he exclaimed at the exotic weed. He accepted the handful Rankin gave as an offering and rolled some of it into a rolling paper. The dread nodded at his decorum since good weed deserves paper, not a cigar. "Sup with Lisa?"

"The gal dem 'pon fire!" he moaned and grabbed his meat through his pants. They both got a good laugh out of it since he'd heard she was burning. She was burning so bad that she was burning dudes by just giving head. "Da gal dem, Reign say that's mi pickney in 'er belly?"

"You asking?" Seven asked since it sounded like a question. "Shit, if you hit, you the only one around here who got that ass!"

He would know, too, as bad as he had wanted Reign. She was play-ing hard to get while the rest of the girls were throwing pussy at him like a rock star. Actually, he was a pretty thug who was getting money and that's a rock star around these parts.

"So...hmp?" Rankin said when he realized he'd been duped. Duped and burned by the pretty Puerto Rican pussy.

They smoked in silence as they both thought about Reign. Seven couldn't believe she'd let ugly Rankin hit when she'd turned him down. Rankin was thinking about going over there and sucking that young pussy inside out.

"A'ight yo," Seven said when Rankin stood to leave. Seven stood, too, to escort him out.

"Next week," he said with desire in his eyes. He didn't even hear Sev-en's reply as he rushed down the hall and hit the steps. He busted out the building to find Reign sitting on his car.

"You not fucking with me no more?" she asked with a pout and bat-ted her eyes.

Rankin got hard instantly but his dick hurt so he winced in pain. "Mi ah busy ya know," he said, trying to be hard. "Ya mother dem 'ome?"

"Nope," she said and hopped off his car.

Rankin looked to make sure she didn't leave a scratch before look-ing at her large ass as she walked away. He knew how clean and sweet it was so he followed her into her building.

"Oh shit!" Unique said and waddled down the hall when she heard her friend coming in. She ducked into the bedroom just as Reign and Rankin entered. She peeked out and saw Reign take off her coat and head her way.

"Keep yo ass in here!" she fussed in a whisper and peeled her sweats off. The girls had plenty of post pregnancy clothes, provided they wore their same sizes. Until then, their wardrobe was strictly sweatpants and shirts.

"Okay," she said but didn't cross her heart because she didn't mean it. In fact, this would be payback.

"I missed that sweet poom-poom," Rankin admitted when Reign returned wearing nothing but a T-shirt. Her big nipples poked through the fabric but were far too sore to be sucked on.

"It missed you, too," she said and meant it and took position on the sofa—that face down, ass up position on the sofa.

"Lawda mercy!" he proclaimed as if her plump pussy was a spiritual awakening. He pulled her butt cheeks open and flicked his tongue like a snake.

"Shit!" Reign shrieked as her whole body jerked from the sensation.

Unique eased out of the room and crept down the hall. She was feet behind him as she began to record. She felt her own box get juicy and squishy as she watched him eat her ass and pussy. Rankin ate Reign to a room-shaking nut and flipped her over for seconds. Unique had enough footage and snuck off.

"You not gonna cum?" she asked when she saw he wasn't pulling on his dick like always. She wasn't worried about his pleasure so much. She just liked to watch cum skeet out his dick.

"Mi good. Just want to please you ya know," he lied. Truth be told, he was afraid his dick might spit flames and set the place on fire.

"Kay," she shrugged and spread her legs. She may have been a kid but she busted a grown lady nut in his mouth. He was actually full after drinking all that juice straight from the tap.

"Here you go," Rankin said and parted with a little over a thousand dollars.

"Thank you," she said and batted her eyes once more.

"When you gone 'ave mi pickney?" he asked. He couldn't wait to get back inside the pretty, young thing.

"Couple months. You still gonna get me a place? My moms said I can't stay here with the baby," she lied.

"Yah, mon. Mi ah put you in a spot. No worries, mon!" he assured her. He leaned in and puckered his black lips up for a kiss.

Reign grimaced and closed her eyes while he planted a smooch on her lips. She wiped it away vigorously as soon as she let him out.

"Dang! That man had you howling!" Unique laughed when she came out. She laughed even louder when she saw her leg was still shaking.

"Girl!" was all she could say. She counted the money out and divided it directly in half. "When he get me this spot, we gonna get his ass and get paid!

"And I know just how we...gone...get...him," she said while connecting her phone to the TV. Once she did, she hit 'play' and started the recording.

"Sss...mmm. Yeah... Eat it... Sss," the onscreen Reign while the real life Reign turned beet red in embarrassment.

"Girl! You recorded us!" she shrieked but kept watching. "Dang, he be eating!"

"Yup, and when he get you the spot, I'ma sneak up just like that and crack his damn cabbage!"

"Word!" Reign agreed. She liked him eating her and loved the money but dude had violated her and he was going to die for it.

"Looking for me?" Lisa asked when she saw Rankin leave Reign's building. She had been posted up since she saw him enter it.

"Ya, mon!" he barked. Just seeing her face made his sick dick throb. He looked around before throwing a straight jab that knocked her straight out.

*****

"Who?" Seven asked but still peeked through his peephole. He saw Mike-Mike and quickly pulled it open. "You done already?"

"Uh, yeah," he replied as Seven turned his back to lead him inside. As soon as he did, he pulled his trusty, rusty .22 and shot him in the back of his head. Seven dropped on the spot while Mike-Mike turned his he gun towards sofa. Luckily, it was empty since Shanasia was still in the room. She knew what was going on and immediately rolled under the bed.

"Okay, okay," Mike-Mike said, trying to calm himself. He spotted the weed on the table and nodded at it. He checked Seven's pockets and came out with close to a grand. That's pocket change for a dope boy so he knew that there was more. It wasn't under the sofa cushions but he did pocket the coins he uncovered.

"What the fuck?" he frowned at the fruity weed. He was used to dirty brownish-green weed so he tossed it aside.

Shanasia huddled in fear when she saw red shell toed sneakers enter the room. He pulled the mattress off and found another thousand dollars. There was a few more thousand in the closet which prevented him from going under the bed. Seven had over a hundred thousand in the apartment but the thirty-five hundred Mike-Mike had was more money than he'd ever had in his life. He snatched a pillowcase off the pillow and stuffed it with stuff he liked. Lastly, the weed went in and he went out the door.

Shanasia waited several minutes after she heard him leave before moving. She peeped down the hall before stepping from the room. She crept forward and peeped into the kitchen.

"Oh Seven!" she moaned, seeing him lying face down on the floor. She cocked her head curiously when she thought she heard him say something. Dead people don't usually talk but she still asked the corpse, "Huh?"

"Call 9. 9...1...1" he pleaded and went back to sleep.

Shanasia hopped right to it and called 911.

"911, what's your EMERGENCY?" the operator asked. She made sure to stress the word emergency because all kinds of people called with all kinds of bullshit.

"My friend got shot in his head! Please hurry!" she pleaded.

"Honey, if he shot in his head, there ain't no hurry," she said sarcastically and started to notify the coroner.

"Huh? But he still alive! He was just talking!" Shanasia begged.

"He is? What's the address?" the operator asked and entered it into the computer, sending fire and rescue rushing in their direction.

"Oh, what now?" Unique asked when she heard sirens pulling on the block. The red flashing lights drew them both to the window to peep outside.

"That's Seven's building! Let's go see what happened!" Reign said, causing

Unique to frown at the concern she heard in her voice. She wanted to see too so she grabbed her coat and followed her outside.

The girls joined the growing crowd of nosey people who gathered to see what happened and to whom. They found Neta and the rest of the crew and joined them.

"What happened?" Unique asked to all but focused on Shanasia since she was Seven's latest girlfriend.

She had an odd look on her face as she scanned the crowd instead of watching the building like everyone else. Her eyes went wide when she spotted the red Adidas. She ran her eyes up his leg and found Mike-Mike when she reached the face.

"I'on know," Neta said just as paramedics brought a stretcher out of the building.

"Is that my baby daddy?" Jewel shrieked when they realized it was Seven. It was mainly for Shanasia's benefit since she was his flavor of the week that had turned into a month.

"Is who your baby daddy?" Unique cracked. Reign just shook her head and tried not to laugh.

"Yo, somebody killed Seven! That's fucked up!" Mike-Mike said, just like he had just practiced upstairs. Everyone knew they weren't really cool so lips twisted at the display.

"He can't be dead if the ambulance got him," Black said. No one was rooting Seven on more than him since the responsibility of the block would fall on him next. That meant he was next to get stretched out on a stretcher.

"Bet it was one of them grimy 170th niggas!" Mike-Mike offered but no one really went for it this time. They had bad blood not war so it didn't make sense. The murmurs went mute when cops started filing back outside.

"Yo, nobody seen nothing, right?" a detective asked as he came out. It was just a formality since he knew no one was going to say anything.

Not to them, anyway.

# Chapter 12

"You seen him?" Unique barked at Shanasia when she returned from the hospital.

"Yeah..." she replied and stopped so they could ask her more questions. The only one she didn't plan to answer was who did it. She didn't even answer Seven when he asked if she saw who shot him. Shanasia said no; not to protect Mike-Mike but to protect the grandmother they shared. Every family has a lowlife and he was hers.

"Well, how is he, stupid?" Unique barked, ready to bite if she didn't like it.

"How he get shot in the head and live?" Reign wanted to know.

"Cuz it didn't go in his head. It hit him at an angle and didn't penetrate his skull," she relayed it to them as the doctors had explained to her.

"Oh," she said since she wasn't quite sure what that meant. He was alive and that's all that mattered.

"Yo, was you over there when it happened?" Unique barked once more. She was hot about anyone seeing him even though she vowed she didn't want him.

"Um, you do know I'm not scared of you, right?" Shanasia asked. Unique may have punked most of the chicks Seven dealt with but she wasn't going to punk her.

"Was you there or not?" Reign cosigned to let her know they were together. "Was you at his crib?"

"I was but I left. I came back down after the po-po showed up," she lied. She may have been lying but still took advantage of the opportunity to take a shot at Unique. "Yeah, cuz the condom broke and he busted all in me! Girl, you know I had to go take a shower."

"Oh really? I thought you would just rinse your mouth out and be good?" Unique asked, sounding sincere. Reign snickered at Shanasia when she twisted her lips and marched off.

"Uh oh," Reign warned when she saw Bryan's car come around the corner. He looked straight ahead as he pulled up to Simone's building.

"He ain't even look our way!" Unique moaned. She saw why when her mother came out a second later. She hopped in his car and off they went.

"Girl, you better go get your damn money!" she urged.

It was needless since Unique had already started in that direction. Reign followed behind as she entered the building and went up the stairs. Unique paused, took a deep breath then tried her key.

"Bitch!" she fussed when the key didn't work. She got frustrated and started kicking the door.

"Chill, Neek! Someone gone call the cops!" Reign warned.

Unique kept kicking until she pulled her away and down the stairs. "I need my damn money!" she whined.

"I know, girl. You know I got you, though. Whatever I get, you get!" her best friend said like a best friend does.

"I know but I need my money!" she pouted all the way back up to Reign's apartment.

"How's that boy doing?" Sharon asked when her the girls came back in. She'd heard about the shooting and hoped for the best since she'd known Seven's mother before she died.

"They say the bullet didn't go in," Reign said, still unsure how that worked. Most times people who got shot in the head had a funeral shortly after.

"Thank God!" she said and paused to do just that with a silent prayer. "I hope someone goes to visit him. He doesn't have any family except his grandmother and she don't leave the house."

"Don't nobody wanna see him!" Unique said since she was hot about her money. Reign nodded her head in agreement with her mother. She knew how boring sitting in a hospital bed could be.

"Well, I'm going to catch another shift. Dinner is on the stove when you girls are ready," Sharon said and headed out the door. Now that she didn't have a man, she immersed herself in her job.

"Okay, ma," both said in reply.

Reign hopped in the window to watch her mother catch her bus. She squinted when she saw a strange exchange between her and Bryan who had just returned to the block.

"Hey there!" Bryan said with a smile as he rolled up and rolled down his window.

"Hmp!" she huffed and lifted her head. Her vagina throbbed when it heard his voice but it didn't run her.

"Don't be like that. Let me give you a ride," he offered and came to a stop. He leaned over to open the door but she kept right on stepping. The bus came and she hopped on and went on her way.

"The fuck?" Reign asked, wondering what she'd just seen.

"What?" Unique asked and rushed over so see could see whatever there was to see. She saw Bryan pull back to her old building and rushed to put her shoes back on.

Reign stayed in the window and watched her friend rush across the street and go inside. She figured Unique would be a while and decided to go on a little adventure of her own. She put her sneakers back on and went down to hail a taxi.

"Where to?" the driver asked when Reign managed to get into the backseat.

"Lincoln Hospital," she replied and sat back.

"You ain't 'bout to have the baby in my car, is you?" he asked, fearful for his interior.

"Nah, B," she said and twisted her lips.

He pulled off the block at the same time Unique knocked on her own door.

*****

"Yes?" Bryan asked sarcastically as he opened the door like it was his apartment.

"I need to grab some of my stuff," she said and tried to push past him.

"You'll have to wait until your mom comes home," he said and blocked her entrance. "Your mother asked me not to let you in."

"Move, nigga! You don't even live here!" she shot back and struggled to get by.

"Obviously you don't live here, either," he said with a dry chuckle that grated her whole soul. "Well, what is it? I'll grab it for you," he offered, still being sarcastic.

"My, um... my,'" she said without telling him it was the money she'd blackmailed out of him. "Just let me get it. Please?"

"What you gonna do for me?" he asked, getting hard over what he hoped she would do. He had the upper hand now and planned to use it to his advantage and take advantage of the kid.

"I'm not doing anything for you!" she shot back indignantly as if she hadn't done anything for him before. She had and loved it until he tried to play her.

Bryan saw he'd gone too far and brought it down, but just a little. "Well, how about I do something for you? Let me eat that sweet pussy and you can get whatever you need to get."

Unique balled her face up so hard it squeezed a lone tear out. She was fuming mad but had no choice. "I'm not doing anything to you!" she said and meant.

"You don't have to," he said for a couple of reasons. First, her mother had just sucked him off before she left and promised to do it again when she got off. Second, it was about control and her giving in meant he won. He stepped aside and let her by.

Unique glanced over to the kitchen as she went to the sofa. Bryan was close on her heels so she would have to let him do what he wanted first. She pulled off her sweatpants and panties and leaned back on the sofa.

"Mm, mm, mph!" he said as he admired her plump pussy behind the bush of pubic hair. "You ever shave this thing?"

"For what?" she shot back since she didn't yet understand the benefit of closely cropped pussy hair. Besides, she'd just grown it a few years back so why would she want to cut it?

Bryan didn't answer and instead spread her lips and took a lick. Unique hissed and arched her back just like he knew she would. He took his time and ate her nice and slow until she shrieked and filled his mouth with her sweet juice.

"What...you...doing?" Unique whined when he kept right on eating. He couldn't reply since the cat had his tongue. She figured it out when she busted another nut in his mouth.

"Bout to get me some of this good pussy," Bryan announced and went to pull his meat out.

"No! You said just eat it!" she fussed and blocked the vagina with her hand.

"Come on. I'll give you a few bucks," he said and thoroughly insulted her.

For the first time, she became disgusted at giving her body away for money. Still, she agreed since it would kill two birds with one stone.

"Okay, but in the bed," she said and pushed him up.

He stood and helped her up. She headed down the hall but passed her old room and entered her mother's room. Bryan knew how wrong it was to fuck the girl on her mother's bed but when she climbed on with her pretty pussy aimed at him, it looked so right.

"Missed...this...good pussy!" he said, working his dick inside.

Unique momentarily let go of the grudge she was holding and moaned as he entered her.

Bryan wasn't lying about missing the teenaged vagina. He was so anxious that he could only get a few strokes in before going stiff and exploding inside of her. Unique smiled to herself feeling him jerk and spasm behind her. She'd always heard good pussy will make a man nut quick and that wasn't a full minute. That meant hers was spectacular.

"Eww, now I'ma be all wet!" she whined. "Can you get me a wash cloth? Make sure it's real hot cuz I'm pregnant."

"Okay," he said, not sure what pregnancy had to do with a hot wash cloth. Nothing really but since it took a couple minutes for the water to heat up, she had a couple minutes to do her thing.

Her first thing was her money. She rolled off and crept passed the bathroom into the kitchen. Simone liked to search her room so she couldn't hide stuff there. She didn't like to cook so the roasting pot was a great hiding place.

Meanwhile, Reign reached the hospital.

"Yes!" Unique cheered when she found her money right where she left it. She eased back into the room to get back on the bed. She spotted Bryan's wallet and quickly dug inside. He was giving her some money so she left the bills and swiped his identification card and social security card. Unique used her mother's pillow to wipe the pussy juice and cum from between her legs with her last free second.

"Hope this is hot enough," he said, returning with a hot, soapy wash cloth.

"Un huh," she said and took it. It was plenty hot on her bare box as she washed away some of his cum. There was still plenty left inside of her but it would have to wait.

"Let me give you something for your pocket," he said and went for his wallet. She froze to see if he would notice the missing items but he went straight for the billfold. He tried her up with a twenty since he had the upper hand. He planned to tell her that, too, if she complained.

"Cool," she said instead of thanks and took the money. It was enough to buy calzones for her and Reign, plus soda and ice cream. She smiled at the sex puddle on her mother's bed on her way out of her room.

"Come back next time your mom goes to work," he said and patted her booty as she left.

"Cool," she said instead of the 'fuck you' at the tip of her tongue. She rushed back to Reign's apartment and used her key when no one answered. She saw the reason when she entered the empty apartment. She called Reign's name then called her phone. "Where you at?"

"Huh? Oh, I had to run out. I'll be back in a minute," she said and walked into Seven's hospital room.

"Now I know I'm dead!" Seven joked and tried to laugh. The hairline fracture to his skull wouldn't allow it.

"Gonna have to call you a cat from now on cuz you got nine lives, yo," she said and came near. She tried to give him a pound but when he got her hand, he wouldn't let it go. Reign shrugged and took seat with him holding her hand.

"Yo, I thought I was outta here!" he admitted. "I got shot in my head. My...head, yo!"

"Who did it?" she asked.

Reign could tell by the delay that he knew so she knew it was a lie when he said, "I'on know. I got hit from behind so..." and left it.

"Word," she said without saying what was on her mind. He got hit in his own apartment so he had to know who he let in. "Handle your business."

"Word," Seven replied and changed the subject.

They spent the next hour chopping it up about some of everything and he still had her hand in hers.

"Yo, I gotta bounce!" she remembered when Unique reminded by calling her phone again. She didn't take the call since she was in his face.

"You coming back?" he asked and batted those brown eyes that got him so much pussy.

"Yes!" she shot back before he got the question mark out.

"Yo, once this is over..." he said, meaning returning Mike-Mike's favor and shooting him in his head. "I'm going down south. You should come with me."

Reign rushed from the room so he wouldn't see the smile on her face. She quickly called her friend back before she started blowing her up. Unique was one of those people who did not take no answer as an answer.

"Girl, I just called your ass!" Unique fussed upon answering. Her stomach was growling and doing flips but she was trying to hold on for her friend.

"I'm on my way home now. You heat up dinner?" she asked as she stepped outside and raised her hand to hail a cab.

"I want calzones!" she said with a pout. She loved Sharon's cooking but had her heart set on Italian food from the pizza shop.

"Order me one. I'll be there by time it's ready," Reign said. It wasn't quite true but gave the impression that she wasn't far. Once they hung up, she finally answered Seven even though he couldn't hear it.

"I would love to come with you! But..." she sighed and thought about all the buts that came with it. She wished she didn't play hard to get when Seven first tried to get her. She left him to Unique and the rest of the block instead of keeping him to herself. There were so many buts she couldn't see past them. "But, I can't."

*****

"Girl, yours about to be cold! Where you been?" Unique demanded when Reign returned.

"I hope you got me pepperoni and ground beef," she said and bit into the calzone. They're better hot but it was still good and stuffed with her favorites.

"Of course!" Unique said and forgot about her question. "Look-it!"

"You got your money!" Reign cheered then squinted suspiciously. "How? I hope you ain't fuck that man again?"

"On my mom's bed!" she shot back proudly.

Reign just shook her head since she had a mouthful of food. Not to mention that Unique had a right to be salty since her mother dissed her over some dude. Never mind that Unique's planned backfired on her. Simone should have chosen her child over anyone else.

"Well..." she shrugged and took another bite. While she chewed, Unique produced another 'look-it'. She held up a finger while she chewed, swallowed, and asked, "What's that?"

"I swiped his ID and social!" she proclaimed. "We just gotta figure out how to use it."

"Word," Reign agreed. They now had the first of what would be many IDs they'd stolen. More sweet licks, but that's another story.

# Chapter 13

Technically, Reign wasn't doing anything wrong but she still kept her visits to Seven to herself. It wasn't hard since Unique was a late sleeper. She could get over there for an hour or so and back before she woke up. Seven asked her again to come down south with him but she still didn't answer. As bad as she wanted to get away from the Bronx, she couldn't, wouldn't, leave her best friend behind.

"Where you been?" Unique pouted when Reign returned home from the hospital.

"To the moon. Duh!" she quipped and held up breakfast from the bodega. Hot pastrami, egg and cheese on a roll killed all other questions even though Reign was rather cute for just going to the corner store.

"Pineapple-orange!" Unique cheered when her friend produced a carton of her favorite drink. The smile on her face confirmed her conviction of never leaving her friend behind.

"Yo, my moms came in?" she asked, looking around to see if she could hear her. Sharon would usually hop in the shower and make breakfast before getting in bed for her next shift. Even Reign recognized the sacrifice she made to keep a roof over her head and food in her belly. That still didn't make her chip in and help but at least she recognized.

"Nah, yo," Unique said and looked at the clock. She knew Sharon's schedule by heart by now and she should have been home.

"Probably picked up another shift," Reign nodded and began to eat.

Actually, Sharon had picked up another man. She and a handsome doctor were currently making googly eyes over breakfast after their shift.

A knock on the door turned both heads.

"Who?"

"Neta!" Neta called from the other side of the door. The urgency in her voice said she either had weed or gossip and she knew they didn't smoke. Unique pulled the door open and in rushed Neta with the news. "Girl, guess what?"

"What?" they both screamed at once.

"They say Mike-Mike robbed Seven! I knew it, too, cuz he tried to fuck me for some weed!" she said, only telling half of that part of the story. She fucked him but he has to toss her a few bucks along with the weed.

"Well, he is Shanasia cousin so I believe it," Unique said and crossed her arms. Reign pressed her lips together tightly so she wouldn't laugh.

"Yeah, plus he the only one on the block who got weed. He selling ounces for twenty-five bucks like it's on sale!"

"Get me four!" Reign said and rushed to get some money.

"Me too!" Unique added and dug a hundred dollars out of her pocket. Neta frowned at the roll of money and wondered how she got it. She could possibly be pregnant after last night and only had twenty bucks.

"I thought y'all ain't smoke no more?" Neta asked as they broke her off the money.

"We don't," they both answered. Then Reign finished up with, "but a deal is a deal!"

She was right, too, because Mike-Mike was easily able to get off the stolen weed at the low prices. It worked for and against him as he got his bread up but shined the light on him. Black wanted to murder him but Rankin told him to wait until Seven got out the hospital.

"Hello, ladies," Sharon sang as she entered as Neta was leaving. They both squinted at her to see what had her so happy.

"Sup, ma?" Reign asked and checked her temperature.

"She met a man," Unique nodded with herself. She'd seen the signs in her own mother enough to know.

"I met a doctor," Sharon corrected. "A single, handsome, funny, professional doctor. Who happens to be white."

"So! Shoot, these brothers ain't talking 'bout a bit...I mean, nothing. They ain't talking bout nothing," Unique said.

"So I'ma have a white stepfather?" Reign asked and twisted her lips at the idea.

"If I have my way you will! I'm going to bed," she said and did just that.

Reign and Unique quickly dressed so they could meet Neta before she came back upstairs since she was so loud. Not to mention that she would tap their weed on the way back. They knew for a fact since they would have, too.

*****

"Seven home!" Reign cheered when she saw him step from a cab. She knew he was on his way since he'd told her so she perched in the window and waited.

"And? Why you so happy about that?" Unique fussed and scrunched her face up.

"Duh, cuz he got shot in his head. I know you don't like him, for whatever reason, but we cool," she protested.

"Hmp!" Unique huffed. She respected it since they were best friends. She came over and watched him get out of the taxi, hug Shanasia and enter his building. "Hmp!"

"You okay, baby?" Shanasia asked and helped him up the stairs.

"Nah," he admitted since he still had a splitting headache. He also had a plan in motion to get payback. Once he got safely inside his apartment, he dismissed her. "Yo, I'ma call you later."

"Okay, baby," she said and leaned in for a kiss. She felt malice on his cold lips when he pecked hers.

Seven locked the door and rushed into his bedroom. He held his breath as he went into his closet and cleared the floor. Once he removed the sneaker boxes, he pried up the floorboard and let out a sigh of relief when he saw his money. Mike-Mike had collected the small change and spending money laying around but missed his stash. He pulled out a quarter brick of coke and replaced the floorboard.

"Who!" Seven called from his bedroom when he heard a knock on his door. Last time he'd opened his door, he got shot in his head so this time he brought his gun. He couldn't understand the mumble though the metal door and asked again, "Who!"

"Black!" he yelled loud enough to be heard. He held his hands up when Seven unlocked the door. "Just me, yo."

"Sup, yo," Seven greeted and peered behind him to make sure. Once he felt secure, he stepped aside and let him in. For the rest of his life he would never turn his back on someone entering.

"Yo, I been holding the weed down with Rankin but we don't have the coke connect. You ready for your spot back?" he asked and lit a blunt.

"Nah, I'm not ready for that yet. Just keep doing what you doing," he said without saying too much. Reef had taught him to never show his whole hand to anyone. Reef taught him things but he didn't live long enough.

"What about the connect, yo? Can't operate on the prices I get," he admitted.

"I'll hook you up with Quan. I'll tell him you my right-hand man so you'll be copping for me," he said so he wouldn't have to reveal Tariq. Seven looked at the blunt when he passed and decided, "I'm good. Just got shot in my head, B."

"By who?" Black asked and cocked his head as if it were a dare. The block had a suspect who had always been suspect but needed confirmation.

"Not sure. I got hit from behind," he said. It was his story and he was sticking to it. Especially since Mike-Mike was about to be dead-dead. "But I got a little work left."

"Let me get it! My people waiting on me now!" he said greedily.

"Just give me...six grand back," Seven said, giving him plenty of wiggle room on the nine ounces.

"Say word!" he said with a smile. He was going to enjoy being the boss. "Now maybe I can bag some of these broads you got."

"B, you can have all of them. Except one, that is," he said, looking at a picture of Reign on his phone.

*****

"Anyway, I heard that..." Reign paused her gossip to see who was making her phone buzz. A quick smile spread when she saw it was Seven. He texted, 'sup big head' and she quickly tapped, 'you'.

"Who that?" Unique frowned and wondered who made her smile. "How you got a dude and I don't know about it?"

"How you know this a dude?" Reign said, twisting her lips. She tried to hold back but busted out laughing. "Cuz me and him ain't never gone hook up."

"Seven! I'on care!" Unique said but pouted like she did care.

"He cute, crazy, get money but I ain't tryna fuck behind you. No telling what you got!" she teased and cracked up again.

"Whatever!" Unique said with a laugh and went back to gossiping. Reign talked to her and Seven while he got ready to meet with Quan.

'I'll holla back', he texted when Black knocked on his door once again. He opened the door for Black who greeted him with the six grand he owed.

"Bet," he nodded at the money. It was just extra since he had plenty to leave and start a new life. It was really a new life since he'd come so close to losing this one. "You ready?"

"I'm ready," Black said and turned back to the door. Seven looked over at his own Benz as they got into his car. Black followed his directions over to Harlem and pulled up to Tariq's pizza shop.

"He's here," Seven said, seeing Tariq's car out front. They went inside so he could hand over the crown. A new king was crowned—for now.

*****

"Sup, cutie pie? I know you ain't smoking but you can still come hang out with a nigga," Mike-Mike said when Reign walked into the bodega.

"And do what?" Reign frowned and looked him up and down. He had done a little shopping with his stolen loot but was still a bum. "Hang out where? With you and yo grandma?"

"Nah, ma. I can get a room. And I'ma eat and beat that pregnant pussy up!" he vowed like a campaign promise.

"I could use some dick," Reign asked and looked around to see who could hear her. "We could go to the Motor Lodge?"

"We can! Get your food and meet me on Ogden!" he said eagerly. He shoved a twenty at her to pay for the junk food she was buying for her and Unique. Unique would have to wait because she had work to do.

"Okay," she agreed, licking her lips as she looked him up and down. She may have been in her third trimester but she still looked good. She paid for the food with his money and kept her change. She glanced up at her apartment window when she stepped out of the store and breathed a sigh of relief that Unique wasn't posted up as usual. The nosey girl usually watched the block like it was a huge TV. She made her way down the block hoping no one else saw her. Someone did, though, as she got into a taxi with Mike-Mike.

"Man, you know how long I been wanting to smash you?" Mike-Mike gushed when they started off towards the local Motor Lodge.

"How long?" she asked, screwing her face up since she'd just recently turned seventeen.

"Shit, like five, six years! Since you and Unique used to wear them matching shorts."

"Bruh, we was like thirteen," she said in disgust. She missed the rest of what he said for the rest of the ride. He paid the driver then rented a room for the night.

"Gone beat this pussy up! Gonna poke that baby all in his head!" he laughed and palmed her butt as they walked to the room.

"Mmhm," she lied and let him fondle. Truth be told, the thought of sex made her queasy. She had to turn Rankin down last weekend when he came over. As a result, he only gave her a fraction of what he'd come to give her. He literally pulled out his stash and peeled off a hundred dollars. She felt more like a prostitute than any time she'd actually let him touch her for money.

"You ever been ate from the back?" he asked as they entered the room. He looked behind them and locked the door.

"Actually, I have. Rankin gave me a band to eat my ass," she admitted since it didn't matter. It wasn't like she cared what he thought of her and he certainly wouldn't be able to repeat it. She almost said more but her phone buzzed with a new text. "Take your clothes off."

"Oh, I am!" he said and began to do just that.

As soon as his pants were off, she unlocked the door. He opened his mouth to ask what she was doing but Seven walked in. The gun in his hand answered the query on the tip of his tongue.

"Step out, ma," he growled at her while aiming at him.

"I wanna watch," she admitted and closed the door. Mike-Mike was a dirt bag and she wanted to see him get what he had coming.

"Watch what? Ain't nothing to watch!" the condemned man barked like a little lapdog talking shit it's one pound body couldn't back up. "I didn't rob you, my nigga!"

"Bruh, you shot me in my head. You know what..." Seven asked and answered by firing at his face. Reign didn't even flinch from the sound of the gun in the small room or the sight of Mike-Mike splattered on the headboard. Seven raised the gun again but she stepped in to stop him.

"Save your bullets, B," she said since Mike-Mike was already in the afterlife and wasn't coming back.

"Let's bounce," he said and tucked the hot gun in his pants.

Reign cheesed broadly when he took her by the hand. She viewed him walking her hand-in-hand to his car as their first date.

"This what I had to do to get a ride in your new car?" she asked when they walked over to the Benz he'd wisely parked away from the parking lot.

"You really pregnant by Rankin?" he asked, ignoring her question.

"No. I was already pregnant when he raped me," she admitted just above a whisper.

"And I'm gonna kill him next!" he shot back and pulled out his phone. He was about to lure Rankin over to the block and do just that.

"What you doing? Un uh, don't do nothing, don't say nothing! I got it. He gone get his. That's on Reef!" she swore.

"A'ight, yo," he reluctantly relented. "So that must be Kidd's kid then?"

Reign pursed her lips and nodded her head. She didn't plan to admit to being pregnant by the kid who killed her brother to anyone. Only Unique knew, and she would take it to her grave.

"Just come with me. You don't even have to pack!" he asked again and pulled to a stop to face her. "I'll buy you whatever you need. The baby, too."

"For real?" she asked and melted under his gaze. "Why you want me to come?"

"One, cuz I told your brother I would always look out for you. He knew this street shit would get him killed one day and made me promise to look out for you," he answered.

"Oh, so it ain't got nothing to do with me?" she asked and twisted her lips wistfully.

"That's one. Two is cuz I been in love with you since we was five," he confessed even though he was too shy to look at her when he said it.

"For real?" Reign swooned and giggled. Then twisted her lips again and asked, "So why you fuck my friend then?"

"Which one? I fucked all your friends cuz they was fucking. You started messing with that nigga Kidd," he said, making her giggle again when his face screwed up with jealousy.

"Mmhm, and that's why you about to have a baby with Jewel. Jewel, though?" she laughed.

"Man, she know good and well that ain't my kid," he laughed. "So no excuses. Come with me."

"I can't. I got my moms and you know I can't leave my girl!" she said, hoping he had answer to persuade her.

He didn't and dug into his pocket. "Here," he said and handed her a large roll of cash. She reached for it but he held on to give the directions that came with it. "I know how y'all blow money but save some to come to Carolina. When you get tired of this... come down."

"Mmhm, you gonna have all them country girls going crazy!" she laughed and tugged on the money but he didn't let it go. They locked eyes and the truth spilled out of her mouth. "Okay. I'm coming. That's my word."

Seven released his grip and put the car back in gear. He ignored her complaints and parked right in front of her building. They both wanted a goodbye kiss but neither moved for it.

"See you tomorrow, B" Reign said and pulled the door handle. She stepped out and looked up for Unique but she wasn't in the window.

"No, you won't," he said as she entered her building and went upstairs.

# Chapter 14

"Yo, who the fuck keep knocking on the door?" Reign groaned when whoever was knocking kept knocking. They weren't taking no answer for an answer and kept knocking.

"Maybe mom left her keys?" Unique said, hoping she would get up and see since it woke her up, too.

"Go see," Reign said so she wouldn't have to.

"She's your mom, yo!" she shot back and flipped over. She pulled the blanket over her head and closed her eyes.

"You so wack," she said and rolled out of the bed they shared. Reef's room was empty but they still stayed together in her room. She snatched the blanket off her as she marched down to see who was still knocking. "Who! What!"

"Yo, Seven told me to bring this over here," the first of the two delivery men replied when she opened the door. Seven obviously threatened them as well as paid them for them to be so diligent.

"What?" she wondered as they brought the huge TV inside her apartment.

"Few more things," the spokesman said and went back down. A minute later they returned with high-end electronics and other household items.

"What you got going on, boy?" Reign cheesed as she looked downstairs and dialed Seven's phone. Her face contorted in confusion when she heard his number was disconnected and didn't see his car. She saw she had a last text from him and read it out loud.

'I'm out yo. This my email. Hit me when you on the way'

"Wow!" Reign exclaimed when it dawned on her that he was gone. "He's really gone!"

"Who was...What in the world?" Unique asked when she came to investigate after using the bathroom.

"Man..." was all she was able to get out since Seven's departure had her speechless. She'd refused to go with him but was slightly salty that he'd left without her.

"That's the same kinda TV Tito had," she said, not knowing it was one and the same. Seven got it when Tito got got and now he passed it on. Tariq was right about kings not living long on the block so he'd vacated the throne and got into the wind.

"I'll be back!" Reign barked in a tone that told Unique not to ask to come with. She pulled her coat over her pajamas and pulled on her boots. Unique watched when she left her building and marched over to Seven's.

Reign got up the stairs like she did before she had a full-sized baby in her belly. She knocked hard enough on the door for it to open since Seven didn't bother to secure it. He'd wanted to burn it down since he was never coming back.

"Yo, Seven? Seven!" she called out into the empty feeling apartment. There was plenty of his grandmother's leftover belongings, leftover from the seventies when she'd bought them, but it was devoid of life. Room after room had been stripped of his most prized possessions and the rest were left for whoever was next.

Seven had put his grandmother on a flight and loaded his clothes, sneakers and money into his car before hitting the road. He was giving New York City the middle finger through his rearview mirror as he left for good. Reef once told him the best way to survive New York was to leave New York. He took that advice and survived.

"Man, I can't believe you left me..." Reign moaned and sank to the floor.

She sat there and had herself a good cry.

*****

"You okay?" Sharon asked when Reign came back from Seven's. Her first question was going to be 'What the hell is all this stuff?' until she saw the distress on her daughter's face.

"Uh, yeah. My stomach was, um, yeah," she said, hoping that would change the subject from the room full of expensive etceteras. It did, because her mother rushed to check her out.

"Hurting how? No spotting? Cramps?" she questioned and sat her child down. She didn't want to be a grandmother at this age but her children didn't give her much choice.

"No..." she said, hoping she didn't go too far from the worry on her face. She was only sick about Seven leaving and nothing could cure that.

Sharon gave her a once over and decided she was okay. "Now, what's all of this? So you following in your brother's footsteps? Huh? You a dope girl now?" her mother wanted to know.

Unique paid attention since she wanted an answer to that same question.

"That boy Seven moved down south. He left all that stuff to us. Me and Neek," she said, putting the blame on both of them, then shifted the balance on Unique with, "They used to talk."

"The one who got shot a couple weeks ago?" Sharon asked with her eyes wide. Even she thought he was a cute kid who had some manners, she also knew he was a dope boy since he was on the block 24/7.

"Mmhm. He said that was enough for him. He gone!" she replied. She wanted to ask her mother and friend if they would mind if she went down south with him but didn't.

"Wow," Sharon said again and went to her room. Her new boyfriend doctor had asked her to move in with him too but she'd had to decline. She now had two daughters to look after as well as the kids they were carrying.

"Say word!" Unique said in astonishment. She couldn't remember anyone who ever left on their own. Most people who left 164th Street for good were buried at Woodlawn Cemetery. It was the block's home away from home.

"Word," she said and sighed. The weight of the Bronx weighed her down so she went back to bed.

*****

"Yo! Guess who got killed!" Neta sang happily when Unique and Reign came outside for some fresh air. She wasn't necessarily happy he was dead but she was the first to spread the news and that's always something to be happy about.

"Who?" they both exclaimed at once even though one of them already knew.

"Mike-Mike! Over in the Motor Lodge!" she cheered. "I heard Seven did it cuz he the one shot him."

"Bitch, Seven don't even live here no more! Don't be running your dick suckers about shit you don't know about!" Reign snapped and nearly snapped her head off.

"See, I heard it was them Puerto Ricans he robbed..." Unique tossed in to help Reign help him.

Reign thanked her with a look and cosigned the gossip. "Word, cuz that's how he had all that weed, 'member?" she asked since Neta knew he had been selling weed for the low-low.

Neta was still stuck for a second from being snapped at a moment ago. She shook her head and shook it just as Jewel and the rest of the girls joined them.

"Yo, them Spanish meda-meda niggas killed Mike-Mike!" she blurted while nodding her head to make it true. "Cuz he robbed them for all that weed he was selling."

"I already know! You late! I been heard about that!" Jewel lied. No one wants to be scooped on some gossip so she ran with it.

Reign and Unique looked at each other as the lie got bigger and truer as it bounced around the small cipher. All these girls were sexing a couple of guys each. They would spread the lie along with their legs over the next couple of days.

"Ooh, here come Shanasia!" Neta pointed as her grandmother's car pulled on the block. They'd just come from identifying the body so it could be buried. Once she walked her grandmother into the building, she came over.

"Sorry about yo peoples," Reign was the first to offer. It was true since she was sorry he was a dirt bag and Seven had to kill him. If it wasn't for him, Seven would still be here, so fuck him as far as she was concerned. She was just smart enough not to show it.

"Thank you," she said, accepting condolences from all her friends. Except Unique, of course, who crossed her arms over her chest and let out a deep sigh as if bored.

"Yo, when you having that baby?" Shanasia asked with a twisted smile that conveyed the rest of the sentiment.

"Soon but we ain't gotta wait. We can fight right now!" she said since she'd heard the threat loud and clear.

"Ain't gonna be no fighting no pregnant chicks!" Neta barked. "If you can't wait, I'll fight you."

"I'll wait. Just know I'm waiting," she told Unique and turned on her heels.

"Now here come this one," Jewel said when Lisa came out of her building. She locked eyes with Unique then looked down at her round belly. It was pretty much the same threat Shanasia had just made.

"Girl, you may just wanna stay pregnant!" Neta cracked and cracked up.

Lisa hopped into a sedan with tinted windows and rode off.

"Sup, mama?" Danger asked when Lisa slid in his passenger seat. He was once called Danger Mouse since he was so small growing up. He wasn't much bigger now but carried a huge gun in his career as a stickup kid. His 'shoot first, ask questions last' attitude earned him the name Danger.

"You, my dude. I got a lick for you," she said and told him all about the new king on the block.

Danger had something for her to lick, too, and pulled it out once she filled him in. He rode around getting mobile head and dropped her back off. They would link up again when the time was right to rob Black.

*****

"Why can't you stay?" Doctor Montague pleaded in a tone that could be either endearing or annoying, depending on the situation.

Sharon chose to find it endearing since she'd just given him a dose of that sweet brown sugar he loved to lick on. He'd just sucked a nut out of her before sliding in and getting one of his own.

"Because I have a child," she said and sighed because she now had two and they both were about to have children of their own. She kissed some of her own molasses from around his mouth since she liked the taste of it.

"She can come, too. We'll be one big happy family!" he said. He was cavalier like that and thought it was possible.

She twisted her lips at the thought of bringing her self-centered child anywhere. The self-absorbed girl really thought the world owed her something. Her mind flashed to all the clothes and shoes the girl brought in and it was obvious she could fend for herself. A nasty thought crossed her mind and she shook her head to shake it off.

"What?" the doctor asked seeing her head shake.

"Huh? Oh, nothing," she said and set off round four to change the subject.

He got a good stroke going while she weighed her options.

In her mind she thought, *I should leave them girls right there in that apartment and do me. They chose their lives, why can't I chose mine? Huh? Why? Why I gotta miss out on life? A man? Huh! Why?*

"Can you give me a few months to get situated, then I can move in with you?" she pleaded. She had done like Reef and Reign and chosen herself over everyone else. It would be pretty fucked up in any other family but why should she suffer for her daughter doing exactly what she'd asked, begged and threatened her not to do and coming up pregnant? No. Hell no. She was about to pursue her own happiness.

"I'd wait a lifetime for you!" he vowed like men in love will do. He loved her eyes, her smile, her attitude and work ethic. The sweet brown sugar was just icing on the cake. He might catch some flak from his white family and friends but fuck them. This was his life and he wanted her in it.

"I don't need a lifetime, baby. Just a few months..." she said since her child was almost due.

*****

"Who?" Black demanded through his door since niggas knew to call before they knocked and no nigga had called so no nigga should be knocking. He strained his face at the weak answer that he barely heard and asked again while peeping through the peephole. "Who?"

"Me!" Lisa called out and waved when she saw the light in the peephole go dark.

Black twisted his lips at her and wondered why she was there. He assumed correctly that she was still chasing that bag since she popped up wherever it went. *It's late so why not get my dick sucked?* he thought and unlocked his door.

"Sup, papi? This my friend Danger," Lisa introduced as Danger stepped out the shadows. The large gun in his hand cast a shadow of its own. Black just shook his head at allowing himself to get caught slipping. Dude had the drop on him and there was nothing he could do about it.

"Come on in," he said and shrugged since it was inevitable. *May as well be cordial*, he decided as he calculated how much he was about to lose. He had plenty of cash on hand but the product out in the streets would still allow him to re-up. He had some cash stashed but nothing like what Reef and Seven put away since neither had his bad habit. Either way, he wasn't coming off his stash. There was enough cash and drugs around to satisfy the average jack boy.

"You been smoking woos?" Lisa asked, smelling the sickly sweet aroma of crack laced weed in the air. She spotted a smoldering blunt and answered for herself when she took a pull.

"Nah, I..." he began to say but gave up when she tasted it for herself. Lisa took two tokes and outed it for later.

"I'ma need all your drugs and money, B," Danger asked from behind the Dirty Harry-sized revolver.

"Okay, I'll..." Black began in attempt to get his own gun but Danger was a pro. He'd learned that lesson in his second stickup turned gunfight.

"Chill, B. Just point her in the right direction!" he ordered.

Black let out a sigh and pointed out where the goods were.

"Look, daddy!" Lisa said, holding up a pistol she'd found under the sofa cushion along with ten thousand dollars.

"Mmhm," Danger nodded knowingly when he accepted Black's gun.

Black knew then what was coming. He had to try him and waited for him to turn his head or at least just blink.

"Ooh!" Lisa cheered when she found another bag of cash in his room. She stuffed his jewelry into her pockets and came back out.

"What you fi..." Danger began to ask.

As soon as his eyes went left, Black made his move. It was a good move but Danger was a pro. He knew the average man could travel five feet in a flash, before a person could get a shot off. That's why he maintained a ten-foot distance.

It was more than enough time and space to actually crack a smile while he took aim. Black turned red and pink when the huge gun splattered his brains on the wall and ceiling.

"Well, that was just dumb," Lisa told the dearly departed and went into his pocket. Danger took aim at the back of her head, then changed his mind. Any chick that could dig in a man's pocket while he's leaking brain matter was a keeper in his world. He lowered the gun and decided to keep her. For now.

Meanwhile, 164$^{th}$ had just lost yet another king. At this rate, they were going to need a queen.

# Chapter 15

"What tha blood clot!" Rankin fussed when he arrived to yet another crime scene on 164th Street. He'd planned to swing through, pick up his bread, drop off some pounds, eat some pussy, then cum on Lisa's tonsils. Instead, the block was buzzing with officials collecting yet another body. He knew them being at Black's building was no coincidence.

"Sup, papi?" Lisa said when Rankin stepped from his car. She was slightly winded from sprinting to get to him before anyone else did. They had made up after he'd knocked her out since she planned to set him up next. She, too, was a salty chick and he would definitely be a sweet lick.

"Whata gwan?" he asked, pointing at Black's building with a nod just as the coroner wheeled him out zipped up in a bag.

"Black got robbed," she said nonchalantly. It was a decent lick even though they didn't find his stash. She and Danger split over twenty thousand worth of cash and product.

"Blood clot!" he repeated. He knew that meant his money was gone and he needed a new outlet for the weed he had with him. There was nothing to see so he turned to go see Reign. Specifically, Reign's big, plump vagina.

"Oh shit, he coming!" Reign said and fell away from the window where she was watching the action.

"Who?" Unique asked, sitting on the sofa watching TV and eating Miracle Whip with a spoon.

"Shabba Ugly," she grimaced and shook her head at his ugly as well as Unique's snack. "I'on know how you be eating mayonnaise from a jar."

"I'on know how he be eating your pussy," she laughed and added, "and it's Miracle Whip, not mayonnaise. That's just nasty!"

"Well, let me get rid of Mr. Nasty Mon," Reign said when she heard the sound of Rankin coming down the hallway. Unique rocked a few times and hoisted herself up. She waddled away as her friend waited then opened the door. She made sure to screw her face up when she opened it. They were a matching set since his face was screwed, too. "Sup with you?"

"Mi a lose more money 'pon dis block, ya know," he sighed and plopped down on her sofa. He leaned back and propped his foot on Sharon's glass table.

"Nah, player. That's for coffee, not shoes," she said, pushing his feet off. "I'm still spotting, so I can't do nuffin. Plus, my stomach."

"Hph," he grunted and contemplated. He knew all the dope boys on the block but wasn't sure which one could handle business. "Ooh ya bruddah dem deal wit?"

"After Seven, and Black? No one. The rest of these dudes are worker bees," she said since that's exactly what Reef used to say about them. "Let me do it."

"Do what?" Rankin asked but his laugh said he understood what she meant and thought it was hilarious. "A gal dem? Nah."

"A girl who was taught by the best!" she said, making her case. It was a good case that fell on deaf, chauvinistic ears.

"Nah. Mi 'ave a deal for you. After you 'ave the pickney, dem we'll see," he said and stood. The night had been a total loss so far since he'd lost his money and distributor when Black got carried away in the bag. He didn't get to suck on the sweet young pussy, either. Lisa would be his last option for the night.

"A'ight, yo," Reign said as she let him out without getting any money.

Unique came back as soon as she heard the door close behind him. "Girl, if he give us the connect we gone be straight!" she gushed since she'd heard every word.

"Girl, we gone rob his ass and be straight anyway," she reminded. She wanted the connect to run the check up before Rankin got himself killed. She knew for a fact that he was about to get killed.

"What's up, yo?" Lisa asked as Rankin stepped from Reign's building and looked side to side, looking for her.

"Ooh at your 'ouse?" he asked, already walking in that direction.

"Um, my moms but..." she said, rushing to catch up with him. She finally passed him when they reached her building and went inside. She used her key and poked her head in. "Ma, I have company."

"Funny but you don't have your own place to have company," she quipped in Spanish and walked her grandson into her room.

"Come on," he said and led him into her bedroom. Rankin was in a foul mood and intended to take it out on some pussy. "Come 'ere!" he demanded and stuffed himself into her mouth until she gagged.

Tears streamed down her face as he savagely fucked her face. She was relieved to feel him grow hard as a brick so he could pull out her mouth. He wasn't any easier on her vagina. Once he worked himself in, he pounded with all he had.

The bedroom door eased open and in walked her son. Her son, not his, so he didn't stop. The child cocked his head curiously as he witnessed his first sex act.

"Go! Go to grandma!" Lisa fussed and ran the child off. He scurried away but left the door open. The sounds of rough sex reverberated throughout the apartment.

"Bumba clot!" he proclaimed and pulled out of her pussy. Lisa knew where he was going, or cumming, and braced herself.

"Argh!" she gagged once again when the tip of his dick touched her tonsils. She had no choice but to swallow the torrent of cum when he came down her throat. He used her mouth to wash the sexual secretions from his dick before putting it away.

"Ere," Rankin said and broke her off a few dollars.

She wanted to complain over the happy meal money but held her tongue. She could wait since he was getting robbed anyway. He could hold on to it until she and Danger came to collect it.

*****

"Man, ain't no weed out this bitch!" Neta grumbled when she saw Reign and Unique waddled out of their building.

"That's what all these sad faces about?" Reign asked, scrunching her face up like something stank.

"Hell yeah. Ain't nobody tryna walk over to the projects for that babbit they selling!" she fussed. Rankin had the best weed in the city

"Ooh! Ooh! I got some weed!" Unique called out when she remembered the few ounces of weed she'd bought from Mike-Mike when he had his fire sale.

"We'll be back!" Reign said and led the way back inside.

Luckily Sharon was out even though she wasn't at work. She spent less and less time at home since she spent more and more time with her man.

Both girls had been bagging weed since Reef started selling years ago. Both had four ounces apiece and could easily bag a hundred bucks in dime bags off each one. Reign knew where a bag of baggies were in Reef's room and quickly retrieved them. A few minutes later they went back down and found a crowd.

"Dang!" Reign giggled at the line for weed. Neta had spread the word up and down the block. She told two friends and they told two friends and word spread like a rumor and rumors spread like a California wildfire.

"Say word!" Unique exclaimed and began making sales. The smile on her face disappeared when she saw her mother fall into the back of the line. "I'll be back."

"Oh, okay," Reign said when she saw Simone. She waved her to the front since she was as pregnant as she was. "Hey, Miss Simone. What you tryna get?"

"Let me get two dimes," she said and passed off a twenty she'd just gotten from Bryan. Unique had managed to avoid them both since she got her money from the house. Her streak was over when her mother copped her weed and headed straight for the bodega where she'd ducked off to.

"Shit!" she said when her mother came in her direction. Her mother had taught her a lot of things in life but being a punk wasn't one of them. She lifted her head and stepped outside as she was stepping in.

"Sup, yo?" Simone asked when they came face to face. "You good?"

"I'm good," she replied. She waited to see if there was more coming but none came.

Simone felt bad about choosing her man over her child but not bad enough to fix it. Her daughter would leave home one day, anyway, so she chose herself.

Unique went back over to Reign and finished selling the rest of her weed. They both sold out of what they'd brought out an hour after they came out. They went to bag the other half to get through the day.

"We need more!" Unique said when they got back inside. It only took an hour to sell the first half so they wouldn't last the day.

"We gone get more!" Reign insisted with a sigh. She screwed her face, picked up her phone and made a call.

"Whata gwan?" Rankin asked when he took the call. He assumed she must have wanted some money since he didn't give her any the last time he came over. She didn't give him any pussy to eat so he didn't break bread. It was his way of training her to realize what he thought of her. She was only as good as her vagina and she understood that loud and clear.

"Come eat me. I'm feeling better," she said, making Unique's eyes go wide. She covered her mouth to conceal a snicker.

"Mi on ma way, ya know!" he gushed and got up.

"Yo, bring me some weed, though. Like, a pound?" she said before he hung up.

"Mi ah bring two!" he said since that was still cheaper than the thousand dollars he usually gave her.

*****

"Wow!" Reign said when Rankin texted from downstairs. He had never been over during the day but Sharon hadn't been home much lately, anyway. According to the new schedule she kept, she had a couple more hours before she came in to change for work.

"He was speeding to come eat that box!" Unique snickered once more as she waddled away. Reign hoisted herself up and opened the door just as he reached it.

"Mi in a 'urry," he advised needlessly since she was, too. She walked over to the sofa and positioned herself for him to eat her from the back. She pulled her T-shirt over her large ass and lunch was served.

"Lawda mercy!" he marveled at the sweet young poom-poom and sealed anus. Her pussy got wet in anticipation of what was coming.

"Sss!" Reign hissed loud enough for Unique to giggle in the back when he licked her asshole.

Rankin scooped some of the juice from her juice box and stoked his dick while he twirled his tongue around her vagina and anus. She almost didn't know which she liked better. She decided on her vagina when he zeroed in on it. His own strokes got the best of him and he busted a nut on the floor.

"I'm...about...to cum!" she stammered.

She wasn't the only one, though, and her mother walked in as soon as an earth shaking orgasm shook her world.

Reign looked up at her mother while cumming in the Jamaican man's mouth. Sharon paused and blinked to process what she was seeing. It was what she saw so she continued on to her room. Just more fuel to the fire that was growing inside of her. A burning desire to start a new life with her new man, no matter who she had to leave behind. Unique had dove in the bed and covered herself with the blanket when she saw Sharon coming down the hallway.

"Ooh dat?" Rankin asked with his mouth glistening like a glazed donut.

"Mi, my mother," she said with her legs still shaking. "You gotta go. Let me get that."

"Ere," he said and passed off two pounds. He quickly put his dick away so he could get out of there. He knew most mothers wouldn't approve of his 38-year-old ass eating their 17-year-old daughter's ass on the living room sofa.

"A'ight, yo," she said and let him back out. She quickly hit her room to put the weed away before going to talk to her mother.

"Did she see you?" Unique asked urgently, still hiding under the blanket.

"Did she!" she replied with a humorless chuckle. "Saw me bust a nut all in his mouth!"

"Oh, wow. Where we gonna stay now?" she whined.

Reign pressed her lips together to keep the truth in. Truth be told, she wished Sharon *would* put her out. She would catch a cab to Penn Station and be on the next thing smoking to Seven.

"Let me see what she talking about," she said and crossed the hall to knock on her door. "Ma? You sleep?"

"No, come in," she said as she slipped on her robe.

"Um, okay. I know you mad, but let me, um, explain," Reign said, stalling to think up an explanation.

"You had some grown man in my house having sex. What is there to explain? My only thing is where, how did I fail so badly? My daughter selling herself. I know you don't go with that man, so he must pay you. That's how you have a room full of new shit in there," Sharon went on. They both noticed that she was piping up as she went along so she pressed her lips together and piped back down. "You can do whatever you want to do. I can, too."

Reign wanted to ask what she meant by that since she could feel the angst when she said it. She decided not to push her luck and eased back out of the room. She took a quick shower to wash the saliva and cum from between her legs then went into her room to bag up the weed.

"One for me, and one for you!" Reign cheered when she pulled the weed back out.

"We 'bout to get rich out here!" Unique cheered when she saw the two pounds.

It wasn't quite enough to get rich off but they wouldn't be broke, either. Until Rankin found a replacement, they were it.

*****

"Yo, let me get some work," a dope boy called Young asked when he came to cop some weed to smoke. He was so used to being fronted weed that it never dawned on him to buy some to flip. He was spending his last ten on a dime bag instead of food, so he swallowed his pride and asked.

"We really ain't holding like that. I can see if we can get more later. Get at me," Reign explained.

"Dang! Err body tryna get on! What blood clot, ras clot, bumba clot Rankin chat 'bout?" Unique asked in her best patois.

"I'on know? He said he got something going on. He been over in Black old building twice today," Reign said, wondering what he had going on. She'd managed to buy two more pounds after quickly selling out the last batch in a few days. Getting caught by the girl's mother was enough to keep him from coming there again but he had something else in mind.

"Guess we'll find out cuz we'll be done by tomorrow," she sighed. Both were finally able to stack some money since they were too busy to spend it. They just sat on pillows on Reign's stoop and sold weed.

She was right, too, because the next day Rankin called her from downstairs. She invited him up but he insisted she come down. Reign let out a deep sigh at having to move. Time was drawing near for her to give birth but even shorter for Unique who was a few weeks further along than she was.

"What's up, yo?" she asked when she stepped outside.

"Follow me..." he answered and started across the street. Halfway across, he noticed she hadn't budged besides crossing her arms over her chest. "Ya wan what ya ask mi fa? Come."

She did want what she'd asked him for so she did come and follow him into the building. She let out a deep sigh when he started up the steps. Still, she wanted what she'd asked for and followed him up. Followed him right into Black's old apartment. It was now done up in new etceteras and furnishings. It was gaudy Jamaican style stuff but still new.

"Who stay here?" she asked, making a face like young girls are supposed to.

"You! Dis your place, ya know!" he said, displaying his ugly smile as he waved his diamond and gold clad hands around.

"What you talking about?" she asked. He said he would get her a place once she had the baby but she envisioned a high-rise somewhere uptown. Not an apartment on her own block.

"Mi get you ah place, ya know. Now I can 'elp you run the block!" he cheered. He would really be helping himself since there was too much money on this block to let it go and the block was too hard on kings to allow a queen. He would hang out over here and oversee her overseeing the block. A win/win for now but even moreso once she had that baby and he could fuck her again.

"Oh, okay. But, my mom, she not gone let me move in with a man!" she reeled.

"Mi ah chat bout dat with 'er once you 'ave da pickney dem," he nodded. "Come look 'pon da rest."

Reign relented and let him show off the rest of the apartment. She twisted her lips since she knew it was his way of trying to get her into the bedroom. She had weed already so she didn't need to let him eat her. She nodded at the nicely appointed kitchen, bathroom and finally, the bedroom. It had a huge bed, TV and dresser but her eyes zoomed in on the large safe. She could see pounds of weed and stacks of cash from the doorway.

"This is dope!" she cheered. She focused on the safe while he stripped her pants and panties off on the bed. She stared into the safe while he poked his thick tongue in and out of her pussy. She paused when he kneeled up and busted a nut on her legs then went back to eating her. She came harder than ever before because the safe turned her on.

"I can't wait to have this baby!" she cheered. Rankin smiled his ugly smile thinking the same thing but for different reasons. She planned to put a bullet in his head and clean that safe out.

# Chapter 16

"Yo, Neek, girl, I know you didn't pee on me?" Reign fussed when she woke up wet. She turned to see Unique sweating and looking crazy.

"I think my water broke?" she asked in confusion. She knew what would happen but now that it was happening she was in shock.

"Ma!" Reign yelled until she remembered her mother was at work. Now she was in a panic as to what to do.

"I gotta go to the hospital," she said and tried to get up. "I need help."

"Hol' up! I'ma get some help!" Reign said even though she was only a few weeks behind her.

She stepped into her sneakers and wobbled down the hall and out the door. A few minutes later, she returned with Tango and Young since they were the only dope boys out on the block. They still looked at her ass as they followed her inside. She led them inside and down to the room they still shared.

"Yo!" Tango said, ready to walk back out when he saw what was going on. "I can't deliver no baby, yo!"

"Nigga, ain't nobody tryna get you to deliver no baby! I need help getting her downstairs so we can get a cab!" Reign snapped.

"Oh, okay. Bet!" he agreed. He and Young went to pick her up but almost dropped her when his hands got wet.

"She peed on herself?" Young reeled when he felt how wet she was.

"Her water broke! Don't you have like six kids?" Reign frowned at his paternal ignorance.

"Seven, but I wasn't there when they was born, yo," he admitted. He was like that fish that skeets on the eggs and keeps right on swimming.

"Ugh!" she grunted in frustration but got them moving. She went to the end of the block and hailed a taxi. "Down the block, we need to go to Lincoln Hospital!"

"You got money, right?" he asked skeptically since that was more important than some kid having a baby. "If not, you can call an ambulance and..."

"I got money, nigga!" she shot back and showed a wad of cash. That got him moving and he drove closer to Unique.

"Her water didn't break, did it?" the driver asked in concern for his interior.

"No," Reign replied and wrapped an arm around her friend. She did her best to comfort Unique on the ride over to the hospital.

"Yo, I'on think I can go through with this!" Unique said when a contraction wracked her whole soul.

"Go through what?" Reign laughed. Even the driver peeped through his rearview mirror to hear the answer. "I hope you don't mean the baby? Too late for that."

"You'll be fine, young lady!" the driver called back as he swung into the emergency room entrance and right up to the door. He even got out to help the passenger-turned-patient out. "Hey! I thought you said her water didn't break!"

"Uh, my bad," Reign shrugged and paid the driver.

They both stepped aside while emergency personal took charge. Unique was wheeled away to go have her baby. She wasn't the only one having a baby tonight.

Reign had just took a seat in the lobby when she heard a familiar voice saying a familiar name. A wide smile spread on her face as her head turned and saw two more familiar faces.

"Just breathe, baby," Bryan urged as he escorted Simone inside the ER. She had a leaned back waddle to her walk as if she were trying to hold the baby inside.

"Wow!" Unique giggled when she realized mother and daughter were having their babies on the same day. It was real funny until the pain and pressure of a contraction hit her, too. She would have blamed it on something else if her water hadn't just broke. "Nuh uh!"

"Are you, okay?" a nurse passing by asked then answered for herself, "No. You're not!"

"Someone need to put this in a book!" Reign laughed as she, too, was carted away to give birth.

*****

"Hey, Sharon!" an ER nurse greeted when Sharon came rushing in.

"Reign Brown, my daughter. She's...having a baby!" she huffed, winded from the sprint from the parking lot.

"I thought that was her!" the woman fawned. She remembered Reign as a pigtailed, snaggletooth child but now she was having one.

"What room is she in? Hope she didn't have it yet," she rambled as she made her way to the maternity ward. She was greeted again by ex-coworkers but all she wanted to know was, "Where's my daughter?"

"Room twelve, Sharon," she was told. She turned around and barged inside to find her child with her child on her chest.

"Here come your grandma,'" Reign sang to her baby when she saw her mother.

"It's early?" she said, making her way over.

"He..." Reign confirmed and turned his little face. Sharon knew something was coming when she locked eyes and announced his name. "Roscoe Brown. Just like his granddaddy."

"Just like your daddy," Sharon said with half a smile.

Reign still hadn't read the letter he'd sent when Reef died. She couldn't because she didn't want to change her memory of him. She preferred to hang on to the tall man who gave her candy and called her princess.

"Just like my daddy," she agreed and cracked a weary smile from just pushing a whole person out of her.

"Well, he's a handsome little fellow!" she gushed over the yellowish baby. She couldn't help not to run faces of light skinned men, teens and boys though her mind to guess which one had fathered him. She was relieved it couldn't the ugly, dark-skinned man she'd found with his face up her ass.

"He is. Yo, guess what?" she suddenly remembered.

"What?" Sharon asked since she couldn't possibly guess. Never in her wildest dreams would she have guessed any of the events of the last year. A dead son, fired from her job, becoming a side chick, a new love and now, a beautiful grandson.

"Unique in room seven having her baby!" Reign cheesed.

"Really? Wow! Same day," she said and kept the rest to herself. She'd half-raised Unique so she knew she was a little fast. The moment of truth was upon them as to whether or not it was her son's child.

"But wait! There's more!" she announced like one of those TV commercials offering two-for-one and free shipping.

"Oh lawd! Not the mother, too!" Sharon exclaimed and shook her head at her good guess.

"Girl, yes! Moms and daughter having babies on the same day!" Reign said.

Ironically, it wasn't the first in this hospital. This was the Bronx, after all. Sex, money, murder and all that.

"Wow, just wow!" she said. "Guess I better go see my other daughter."

"And grandchild, ma," Reign tossed out since she knew her mother well enough to know her leaving that part out was intentional. She'd seen the video of Reef and Unique enough to firmly believe her friend was pregnant by her brother. If he'd fucked her raw once, he'd probably fucked her raw twice.

Truth be told, he'd fucked her raw every time.

"Mmm," Sharon said, meaning, 'we'll see about that', and left the room. She'd worked here long enough to know which way room seven was and headed over.

"Hey, Sharon," a nurse greeted with a question when Sharon poked her head inside.

"That's the grandmother!" Unique smiled when she saw who it was. The answer put another question on the nurse's face since she knew the patient's mother was giving birth as well. The whole hospital knew. "His father's mother."

"Yeah," Sharon said but still meant 'we'll see about that'. She approached and her knees buckled when she saw the little brown face.

"You okay, ma?" Unique asked when Sharon had to grab the bedrail to keep from falling.

"Oh my God! He looks just like Reef when he was born!" she gushed and commandeered the baby.

"He do," Unique nodded proudly and proclaimed, "I named him Reef. Okay?"

"Of course it's okay! Yes, name him after his father. Reef Brown. Last name, too!" she insisted.

"Yes ma, last name, too," she said since it was already on the birth certificate. She laid back and watched the grandmother love on her grandson for a few minutes.

"These are some beautiful babies," she said and shed a tear.

They were but not beautiful enough to stop her from doing what she had to do. To stop her from doing her.

*****

Back in the good old days when Sharon was born, mother and child would stay in the hospital for a week. When Reef and Reign were born they stayed a couple of days. Now, Reign and Unique were discharged along with their healthy baby boys the next day.

Simone had given birth to a beautiful little girl Bryan named Judith after his mother. He still hadn't moved in but without Unique and Sharon, he was able to spend more time and, more importantly, money with Simone. He pulled the car around to pick her up and the three mothers came face to face in the lobby.

"Oh, so you had your baby, too, huh?" Simone huffed like she was tough even though she wanted to see her grandbaby.

"His name is Reef," she said and leaned the baby so she could see. She was ready for her mother to ask her to come home. She loved Reign and Sharon but would have gone. It *was* home after all.

"I had a girl. Another girl," she sighed. Girls start off easy enough, then they grow up.

"Okay, that's what's up," Unique said. She'd left the door open for her to ask her to come home but Simone kicked it shut when she turned to leave. Bryan ignored her until he'd helped Simone into the car. Once the lane was clear, he blew her a kiss and winked his eye.

"Laugh now, nigga," Reign snarled. He was another one on her list of people who needed to get theirs. She would gladly give him what he had coming.

"Could have gave us ride. We going to the same damn block!" Unique fussed as they pulled away. She raised a hand and hailed a taxi.

"164 and Ogden," Reign told the driver as they got themselves and their children situated. Once they were all buckled up, they made the trek across town and up the hill.

"Uh oh! Look at mamacita and mamacita!" Neta sang out as she saw the girls getting out of the taxi. She led the way over to see the newest additions to the block.

"Hurry up. I don't want this bitch breathing weed and dick breath on my baby," Reign said before they reached them. Then switched to, "Sup, chica? We'll be down later."

"Mmhm," Unique cosigned.

They paid the driver and rushed inside. Not fast enough for Rankin not to see, though. He began calling before she could get to her apartment. He sent a text when she didn't answer.

"This nigga talking 'bout, let mi see mi pickney. Let me borrow your baby," Reign said.

"I am not!" Unique laughed. "You can take a picture of him but I'on want that man scaring my baby. Reef a day old. That's too soon to put that much ugly in his life!"

"You stupid!" she giggled but did just that. She snapped off a few pics and sent them across the street to Rankin. He texted a second later and cracked her up again.

"What?" Unique asked and chuckled along with her. Reign was laughing so hard that tears began to stream from her eyes. "What?"

"Girl, he said... He look just like me!" she finally managed to get out and cracked up again. She laughed for ten minutes straight off of that before she was able to read the next text. "I'll be back. He said come get some money!"

"I'll babysit! Go get that bread, yo!" Unique urged.

Reign left out to do just that. She just missed Sharon when she went into his building.

"Where's my daughter?" Sharon asked, clearly hot about the new mother not with her new baby.

"She ran to the store," Unique said while switching from social media to text and telling Reign to stop by the store and why.

"Oh, okay, cuz I promise; no, swear. I swear I'm not babysitting one baby for one second!" Sharon vowed aloud as she'd vowed to herself from the moment her child popped up pregnant. They'd managed to squeak through the school year so they would have to enroll in the special school that specialized in teen mothers. They would bring their babies to class with them.

*****

"Whata gwan! Let mi see mi pickney!" Rankin cheered when he opened the door for Reign. His smile dissipated in an instant when he saw her arms were empty.

"You know I can't bring no newborn baby outside!" she fussed. "You can come see him later. My mom home now."

"This you 'ome now. Bring ya tings and move in," he insisted. She'd agreed to do just that once the baby was born and now he was born.

"I can't just up and leave like that. Let me work on my moms for a minute," she placated. "I need some money, though, cuz he need everything!"

"No worries," he said, stuffing his hand into his pocket. It took some doing because it was full of cash. Working the block himself cut out the middle man and ran the check up. "'Ere."

"Wow!" Reign couldn't help but shout when he extended the cash. Five thousand looks like twice that when it's broken down into street bills.

"Make sure 'im 'ave err ting 'im need!" he proclaimed proudly. Rankin was a lowlife but took pride in taking care of his kids. All fourteen of them, from the Bronx to Kingston.

"Okay...baby," she managed to get out then turned to get out.

Rankin had other plans in mind. "Mi ah wait long time fa ya to birth tha pickney dem," he said and licked his thick, black, rubbery looking lips. He gripped his meat through his pants and said. "Time fa put 'tis back in ya."

"Bruh, I just, had a baby! Got stitches and the whole nine!" she shot back incredulously.

"So?" he shrugged since his last baby mama fucked on her first day home from the hospital.

"So? The doctor said six weeks is so!" she shot back. "I'll see you then!"

"Hmph?" Rankin said curiously as she walked out of his apartment.

He shrugged it off since he still had Lisa to take his frustrations out on. He hit her up and told her to come over later. She agreed and offered to bring a friend.

"Oh shit!" Reign said when she almost went home without going to the store. She detoured and hit the bodega for snacks. As an afterthought, she picked up diapers and formula for the kids. The hospital gave them the teen mom starter pack that would last a few days. She also bought a blunt since she was no longer pregnant.

"I'm glad you know that one of you must be home at all times!" Sharon began as soon as the door opened. Reign looked down and confirmed she hadn't yet stepped one foot inside the apartment. She looked to Unique who gave a warning with her eyes to say 'ma is on one today'.

"'Kay ma," she said and came inside to close the door. Reign knew from experience to just agree when her mother went on one of her tirades.

"I'll watch my grandsons once. Just once, when you girls go get WIC, welfare, food stamps and everything else. I took care of my kids. By myself! Wish I would take care of y'all kids! Shit, I wish I would! Working like a Hebrew slave and..." she rambled on and on.

Most of it was true but some of it was guilt for what she knew was coming.

Reign saw her name on an envelope in the stack of mail her mother had just brought up and reached for it. The return address was from Clinton Correctional Facility and she heard her father's voice call her princess. The sweet memory was erased when she saw Kidd was the sender. She tuned her mother out and retreated to her room.

"Okay, think it's a joke. Walk off while I'm talking like I ain't talking about nothing. I got something for your ass. Watch!" Sharon fussed to her back.

# Chapter 17

*Deer rane dis me kidd. I sory abote yor brother an my brother. day sent me to prizin but i only got tin yeers. I herd you is pregnit and i no it my. wen i com home i want us get marred togetha. I need you to sind me som muney cuz my moms bi bugin. ok i love you. rite me back OK.*

"What the fuck?" Reign fussed when she reached the end of the letter. She looked over at their son and so many emotions flashed through her mind. First, the letter was funny as hell. She pictured him writing words exactly how they sounded to him. Then he was the father of her child. The sweet, pretty little boy sleeping soundly in his little bassinet. Then the flash of anger outweighed everything else.

"Fuck nigga killed my damn brother and he talking about let's get married! Send him some money! Oh, I'ma send you something a'ight!" she snapped and got to writing a letter of her own. She transcribed her thoughts and addressed it right back to Clinton Correctional Facility.

"You okay?" Unique asked when she came in the room and saw the mask of anger on her friend's face.

"No!" she admitted and filled her in.

"Wow! He crazy!" she cosigned and climbed in bed. She'd already learned to sleep when her child slept because there was no sleep when he was awake. Reign sealed up her letter and joined her in sleep.

"I'm going back in to work," Sharon announced when she stuck her head in. She told them where she was going but not where she was going after. She and her doctor friend had a date under his sheets before she came back to check on the new mothers.

"Okay, ma," Unique replied first and shook her sister. "Reign?"

"Huh? Oh, you out, ma?" she said and looked to her own child. She breathed a sigh of relief that he was still sleeping.

"Yeah, I'm out. Make sure to change them and keep them on their feeding schedule. Neither one of you need to go anywhere! I mean that," Sharon fussed and fussed her way out the door. "Not that you gone listen anyway..."

"Yo, moms real extra lately," Reign spat when she heard her mother leave.

"It's more than that. Something up with her," Unique said since she paid attention to detail. The woman was fed up and she could tell.

"Anyway, let's feed these babies so we can get high!" she said and went to fix some bottles and roll a blunt.

The new mothers followed directions and cared for their new-borns. Maternal instincts helped them along the way as they played ba-by doll with real babies just like they when they were little girls. Once the boys were clean, dry and full, they put them back in their little beds and met back in the living room.

"Now!" Reign announced triumphantly and held up a blunt.

"We deserve it!" Unique cosigned and lit her lighter. She held the flickering flame under the cigar and Reign inhaled deeply. She took two tokes and passed as is standard in any hood.

The few months without smoking took its toll on both girls and they struggled to even finish. Reign nodded off midway through and began to snore. Unique heard her friends below and decided to share. She opened the window and called out.

"Yo, Neta!" she yelled, causing Neta to look up. "Here!"

Neta caught the blunt out of the air before it hit the ground. She immediately took a toke and nodded her thanks while holding the smoke inside.

Unique nodded back and started to pull her head back. She paused when she spotted Lisa and a hooded figure enter Rankin's building. She shrugged it off and leaned down next to her friend and joined the snor-ing contest.

"Ooh dat?" Rankin barked in response to the knock on his door even though he already knew. That's why he pulled it open with one hand and held his dick in the other.

"See you was waiting on me, huh?" she said and pushed in before he could look out. She pulled it closed behind her but didn't lock it. Rankin was old school, though, and locked it himself.

"Suck 'pon tis," he ordered and tried to pull her head down to where his dick was.

"Chill, papi. Let's go to the room so I can stretch out and relax," she purred and petted the head of his dick like it was a puppy. Every man knows chicks give better head when relaxed, so he led her to the bedroom.

Lisa stifled a smile when she saw the safe was open. Her pussy got super wet from seeing the dope and dough within. Chicks give good head when they're happy, too, and the sweet lick definitely made her happy.

"Bumba clot!" he cheered when he felt her tonsils on the tip of his dick. He was content with that good throat until he reached down and felt the puddle between her legs. He pulled her up by her ankle and switched holes. This one was as good as good the last so he repeated, "Bumba clot!"

"That's, right... get, it!" she urged as he got it. He pounded until he went stiff and filled her up. "Mmm, that was good. Let me up. I'ma get a wash cloth and clean it off so I can suck it again."

"Ya mon," he agreed since it ended with him getting his dick sucked again.

He squinted at the memory of how much she enjoyed sucking her own juices off him. He leaned up at the sound of her footsteps passing the bathroom. Then hopped up when he heard the front door open. He rolled off the bed and went for his gun but it was too late.

"Nuh uh!" Danger warned from behind his huge gun.

The barrel looked like he was staring into the Holland Tunnel. Rankin's arms slowly rose in defeat. All eyes went to the open safe. Two faces smiled and one did the opposite. There was too much money in there to lose and Rankin just couldn't live with it. They could have the cash and weed that was laying around but not his stash.

"Can't 'ave mi money!" Rankin shouted and made a dash for the safe.

He made it two steps before Danger put two slugs in his back. The force from the shots slammed him against the safe door and slammed it shut.

A smile spread on Rankin's face as he used his last breath to repeat, "You can't 'ave mi money."

"Shit!" Danger fussed and pulled the body away from the door. He tugged on the handle but it was locked tight. In desperation, he leaned his ear against it and turned the knob.

"What the hell are you doing?" she asked at the idiot attempting to crack the safe like an old cowboy movie. She really couldn't talk because her idea was just as foolish. "Shoot it!"

"Oh yeah!" Danger said and smiled like it was a good idea.

He took a few steps back and fired a round at the safe. The bullet bounced off and hit him right between his eyes. He turned his head to Lisa like he had something to say but dead men tell no tales. He dropped like he was hot and died on the spot.

Lisa stood there for several minutes trying to figure out what she'd just witnessed. She frowned down at Rankin with his cum running down her leg then over at Danger who still clutched his own murder weapon in his hand. It would be funny if not for all the money behind door number one. She was so close, yet so far.

She put her ear against the safe and dialed the knobs, too, but didn't hear a thing. There was no way in so she took her time and gathered everything of value that she could find and stacked it at the door. That included the money in Rankin's pockets and jewelry from his body, a couple pounds of weed from the kitchen and few thousand under the mattress. She even went into Danger's dead pockets and cleaned them out, too. Coins, keys and all.

"I'll be back for you guys," Lisa told the huge TV and electronics as she loaded her loot into bags and departed the apartment. She had Rankin's keys to come and go until there was nothing else left to come for.

*****

"Up! Get up! Reign, Unique! Get up and get dressed!" Sharon fussed and shook the girls awake when she returned the next morning.

"What, ma? Dang!" Reign fussed back while Unique got right up and looked at her baby.

"Only dang in this house is danger! Now watch your mouth. Get up and get dressed!" she barked.

"Okay, ma!" she relented but still had a little too much on her voice. Sharon let her know by raising one eyebrow so she took some off and asked, "What's going on, mommy? The babies are sleep. They fed and dry."

"And you both need to get down to that office and apply for everything those people will give you. Stamps, a check, um, Medicaid, WIC, the works! I'll watch these babies until you get home. That's it, though. I'll never babysit again! That's my word!"

"Come on, Neek," Reign sighed. She showered, dressed and Unique followed suit.

"You need money for the bus?" Sharon demanded once the girls were dressed and ready to leave. She sat comfortably on the sofa between her grandbabies.

"No," Reign shot back sarcastically since she has almost ten thousand dollars hidden in her room.

"Okay. I know how the system works. Say what I said and you girls can get help today. I'll pay half the rent and you two will pay the rest. I'm serious..." she fussed as they left the apartment. "Okay. Think it's a game. Watch... Okay."

"Let's go watch a movie," Reign suggested when they reached the street.

"Movie? Yo, we better go do what your moms said to do," Unique warned. She was a guest and intended to do what she was told. It was her who washed dishes and cleaned up behind her and Queen Reign.

"Man..." Reign grumbled but compiled. She was above taking the bus so she hailed a taxi once they reached Ogden Ave. She complained the whole ride over and the whole walk inside. "Be up in here with all these broke broads!"

"You bugging, yo," Unique remarked as they took a number and took a seat. It was eight AM when they sat down and two PM when their numbers were called.

Both girls said what Sharon said to say and showed their documents. Just like Sharon said, they left out with enough government assistance to live on. Good thing, too, because they were going to need it.

"Shoot, I should hit Shabba Ugly up for some more money," Reign said when they reached the block and saw his car hadn't moved.

"Girl, you still leaking placenta, talking about letting him eat you?" Unique grimaced. Her eyes locked on Bryan coming out of her mother's building and that shut her up.

"Mmhm!" Reign laughed. She led the way inside their building and up to the apartment.

"Well?" Sharon demanded as soon as they stepped inside.

"Well, we're officially welfare recipients!" Reign cheered sarcastically.

"Chill, yo," Unique warned since she had a little more insight. Something was up with the woman and Reign wasn't paying attention.

"Good. Like I said, I'll pay half the rent. You're on your own after that," Sharon stated with an eerie conviction. She kissed her grandsons and stood. She went into her room and came out with two bags and bid them farewell. "Peace!"

"She out, yo!" Unique said when she caught on. "Out, out. Like, not coming back, out."

"Out where? Out what?" Reign laughed. She grabbed a butter knife to open her mother's room but found it wasn't locked.

Her face screwed up when she saw it was almost bare. The two bags were the last of her personal affects that she'd slowly moved over to her boyfriend's house. Her children did whatever they wanted to do and now it was her turn.

*****

"Yo, why this ugly nigga won't return my texts?" Reign asked. She'd moved into her mother's room and sprawled out on the queen bed. Unique took over her old room but they still hung out on the large bed just like they did when they were little girls.

"Call him," Unique suggested. She enjoyed having her own room again, especially since she had all of her clothes in her closet. Something she couldn't do since she and Simone had begun wearing the same size.

"Nah, his voice ugly, too!" she laughed but was fronting and called him. "Straight to voicemail?"

"His car was still there earlier," Unique said and went to go check again. She peered out and saw that the space that his car had been parked in earlier was now vacant. She was just about to report what she saw until she saw something else to report. Rankin's car pulled on the block and parked in front of Lisa's building. Her head cocked sideways in curiosity when Lisa hopped out the passenger seat and Young came from behind the wheel.

"Yo, Reign! Look-it!"

"What the fuck?" she asked as Young retrieved a hand truck from the trunk. They headed over to Rankin's building and went inside. She hopped up and went to get dressed. Unique knew she couldn't go so she stayed in the window to see what she could see. What she saw was

Young and Lisa leave out shortly after they entered. They would come back and attempt to move the safe when the sun went down.

"They left back out!" Unique reported when she came back. "I seen them there the other night."

"Mmhm. Nigga don't wanna return text! Sending me straight to voicemail!" she grumbled on her way out as if Rankin were really her man. She was really hot when she stormed out of the apartment.

Reign had more than just Unique's eyes on her as she marched across the street and into the building. She could feel her stitches as she took the steps two by two. Even though she had a key, she still chose to knock. When she didn't get an answer, she got up the nerve and let herself in.

"Eww!" she grimaced when the unmistakable stench of death reached her nostrils. Rankin and Danger had been there for days and were definitely ripe. A sinking feeling sank in her soul when she looked around the stripped apartment. "Yo! Rankin!"

Reign covered her nose and went into the back. She'd seen enough dead bodies in her life to know in an instant that she was looking at two more. She put two and two together when she recognized the hand truck Young just took out the trunk. She multiplied it by the locked safe and found her answer.

"Nasty bitch!" she fumed. Lisa had beat her to the punch but she had one last trick up her sleeve. She locked the door behind her and headed back downstairs.

"Where she going?" Unique wondered aloud when she saw her friend pass the bodega towards Ogden Ave. She smiled when Reign entered the pizza shop since she was hungry.

"Yo, let me get four slices. Extra cheese!" she ordered and added the cheese as an afterthought. The clerk popped the slices in the oven while she stepped out and got on the seldom used payphone.

"911, what's your emergency?" a bored operator yawned into the line.

"Really?" Reign asked of the inappropriate yawn. "How about a dead body? Or you too sleepy?"

"Well, ain't much of an emergency if it's dead," the sarcastic woman shot back. She did ask for the address and entered it when Reign gave it up. She collected her food and went back home.

"Pizza!" Unique cheered when she came in until she saw the long face. "What happened? What's wrong?"

"Rankin dead. Him and some other nigga laid up stinking in his bedroom," she said sadly. She could give a fuck about him. It was the money she was mourning. "That bitch Lisa had something to do with it."

"How you know?" Unique asked, wide-eyed with fear. She remembered the girl's threat about killing her if she had Reef's baby and she'd just had Reef's baby.

"Cuz, she did it. And they had that thing you move stuff with. It was in the apartment," she said. She wondered if Young was the shooter and who the other man was. All she knew for certain was that Lisa had just cost her a bunch of money. And she was certain of one more thing. "I'ma kill that bitch."

"Cops just pulled up to his building," Unique informed since she kept watch on the block. Reign wasn't surprised since she was the one who called.

Lisa watched, along with the rest of the block, when the first cop car pulled up. Two beat cops went inside to find the crime scene. They called it in and soon the block was hot and swarming with official vehicles. The first thing the cops needed to figure out was what the fuck had just happened here.

"Okay, I see! I get it," a detective chuckled as he examined the crime scene. He pulled his phone and pulled up the camera. "This dude here shot this other dude in the back when he wouldn't open the safe, and..."

"Don't tell me he tried to shoot the safe to open it?" the second asked and joined the laughter. They called the other cops and CSI in to join the laughter. They all had a good laugh at the expense of the dead men before getting back to work.

"So, the third or fourth assailant brought the hand truck to cart the safe away. Make sure to run it for prints and DNA," the first one ordered.

"I'm surprised no one put their ear to it and tried to crack it," the second cop cracked and cracked them up once more.

"Like with a stethoscope!" a lady cop howled while taking pictures of the dead men.

"Stankin Rankin and Danger Mouse," a homicide cop said when he came in and took one look at both men. Both had been suspects in several murders so he was very familiar with both. He leaned in and reminded them both that, "What goes around comes around."

"I'm dying to find out what's in this safe!" second cop gushed since not a crumb of weed or coke was found.

"He beat you to it," his partner laughed, pointing at Danger, who really did die trying to find out what was in that safe. The laughter died down enough for the coroner to remove the corpses. Half the block was outside waiting to see who got killed while the other half watched from their windows.

# Chapter 18

"What's going on out here?" Lisa asked extra loud so everyone would hear. She figured if they heard her asking, they couldn't say she knew.

"This bitch!" Reign growled and locked eyes with her. If looks could kill, both would have tipped over dead on the spot. Unique had gladly stayed upstairs with the kids while she mingled in the crowd to see and hear what was being said.

Reign listened to the murmurs to try and figure out who the second man was. Young was Tango's right-hand man but that wasn't Tango stretched out next to Rankin. A hush fell over the crowd when the safe was carried off and carried away.

"This bitch just cost me all that bread," Lisa growled as they locked eyes. The beef brewing wouldn't be quenched until one of them was stretched out.

She felt nothing seeing two men removed in body bags even though she still had residue from both of them inside of her. She did feel all kind of ways when she saw them leaving with the safe. Lisa knew Reign had to be the one to report it since she'd watched her enter the building and leave shortly after. Now, all of a sudden the cops were here. All she knew was she'd just cost her a lot of money.

"I'ma kill that bitch!" Lisa vowed once more as she watched Reign go back into her building.

"What they say? What's going on?" Unique asked when Reign returned. She was feeding her son so she came over and took over.

"Man, Lisa had something to do with it. Her and Young after we put him on," she said and twisted her lips at the loss of the money. She would have been *really* hot had she known there was two hundred thousand dollars in the safe.

"So who was the other person? I saw two body bags," Unique asked.

"I'on know," Reign replied, leaving out the part about not caring. All she knew was that Lisa was involved and she was going to get hers.

154

"I can't believe moms really left us," Unique sighed again.

"I don't see why not. Your mom put you out over some nigga," Reign reminded. She heard how harsh it sounded once it was in the air but it was already in the air so she left it.

"Yeah, you right. I'm going to bed. I'll holla," she said and took her baby to her room.

Reign stayed behind and sent out an email to Seven.

"Sup big head..."

*****

Unique finally ventured out since it was her turn to go get diapers. She looked both ways when she stepped out like she was crossing the street. She wasn't looking for cars, though. She was checking for Lisa. She spotted her heading into the bodega she was heading for herself and headed on over anyway.

"I heard you bitches had your little bastards. What you name yours?" Lisa dared and gripped the beer bottle like a weapon.

"I named him after his father," she said meekly, down to the floor. Her head slowly rose along with her courage and she said, "Reef Brown. Junior, after his father."

"Oh, you thought I was playing, huh?" Lisa growled and moved on the girl.

"Not in here! Take that shit up out of here or I'm calling the po-po!" papi behind the counter demanded.

"Let's step outside, yo," Unique offered and backed out so Lisa couldn't sneak her.

"So what's up, then?" Lisa barked once they hit the sidewalk. She brandished the bottle like a club, ready to strike.

"Not here. I'on want no one to break it up. Let's hit the roof and get it on," Unique said.

"Word. So yo home girls can't try to jump in," she agreed and followed her into her and Reign's building. Lisa fought the urge not to snuff her and beat her on the steps. She decided to wait so no one would be able to stop her since she planned to kill. A promise is a promise after all.

"Here we go!" Unique said as she stepped out onto the rooftop. Lisa stepped out behind her and heard the door shut behind her.

"What the fuck!" Lisa said when she saw Neta slam the door. She knew what it was when Shanasia, Debra and finally Reign came out from their hiding spots. Jewel was still pregnant so she got some practice and watched the babies. "Let's get it then!"

"Let's!" Reign smiled and passed Unique her bat so she could match her friends. Lisa went for hers but was no match for five girls with bats. They beat her to within an inch of her life before Unique stopped the attack.

"Remember you said you was the flyest chick on the block? Well, we 'bout to see!" she announced. Lisa screamed in pain from her broken bones when the girls picked her up. They carried her to the back ledge and tossed her over.

"Don't look fly to me!" Neta called to her on her way down.

"Not fly at all," Reign agreed when she got splattered in the alley.

*****

"What?" Unique asked since she knew her friend well enough to know something was wrong with her best friend.

"Nothing," she said then said plenty of something. "Seven got a house. And a barbershop."

"You talked to him, huh?" she asked the obvious. "Bet he driving them country girls wild!"

"Probably, but..." Reign said and paused so her friend could ask.

"But what?" Unique took the bait and asked again, "But what?"

"He want me to come down there. To be with him," she admitted.

"So go! I'on care!" Unique shot back but contradicted herself by pouting.

"I'm not going anywhere without you. That's my word!" Reign declared. "We can get an apartment for you. We can go to school like we said. Seven said he'll open a salon for us and..."

"No, go. I'll be okay. I'ma stay right here," she huffed and stormed off to her room.

"Okay. I will!" Reign called after her. She shot a glance over to make sure she didn't wake her son. A tear escaped her eye and ran down her face at the painful thought of leaving her friend. The thought of being stuck on this block forever was even more painful so she got up to get packed.

Reign wasn't sure if she could go through with leaving her friend but started pulling her clothes out of the closet anyway. If she hurried, maybe she would be in Carolina before she thought about it. The clothes were all new so they were all going. Shoes, too, so she started pulling them out next.

"I'ma need more suitcases!" she giggled when she ran out of room halfway through her packing. She removed the last of her shoes and noticed a loose floorboard. She cocked her head curiously at the memory of her brother always sneaking in and out of their mother's room. She leaned down and picked up the board then fell away in shock.

"Neek! Yo, Neek! Come quick!"

"Don't worry, I'm packing. I'm going back to my... What's wrong with you?" Unique asked and twisted her lips at her needing help from her and leaving her, too.

Reign couldn't speak so she just grunted and pointed towards the closet. Unique twisted her lips to the other side and peered in. She blinked, rubbed her eyes and blinked some more but the money was still there.

"How...much is...it?" Reign asked but kept her distance as if afraid of it.

"I'on know..." Unique replied but didn't go near it, either. Reef's voice during pillow talk came to her and she said, "A quarter mil. That's two hundred and fifty thousand dollars!"

"More like one twenty-five each," Reign said and rushed in to grab it. She removed bundle after bundle of bundled cash and passed them back to Unique. She made neat piles on the bed until it was all out. Reign pulled out some weed and another gun and put them on the bed as well.

Reign and Unique looked at each other for a moment then took a deep breath. They exhaled and got down to counting the money. Reef had given Unique a tally a couple of weeks before he passed on so the count was closer to three hundred thousand. It still split the same fifty-fifty and each girl had almost one hundred fifty grand.

"Now what?" Unique needed to know. She had plenty of money but no idea what to do next.

"I...I still want to go. I wanna get off this block! Out this city! Nothing here but sex, money and murder. I wanna go with Seven. Please? He promised Reef he was gonna look out for me. A promise is a promise, you know?" she reasoned. It must have been reasonable since Unique began to nod, too. "What about you? What you gonna do?"

"I'm coming with you! We can get a place. I'ma get me one of them country boys and go back to school. We gonna open our own salon!" Unique cheered and sold her friend on the idea.

"Hell yeah! We gonna call it...Sweet Licks!" she agreed and hit Seven to see that he did too. He did because he wanted to get his girl.

These two salty chicks finally hit a sweet lick.


THE END

# Epilogue

"Mail call!" an officer at Clinton Correctional announced. Most men gathered around whether they got mail or not. Some hadn't received letters in a decade or more while others never got any but never lost hope.

"Roscoe! They calling you!" an inmate called out to the large man doing pushups.

"Me?" he asked, pointing at himself. The officer answered by calling his name for a last time. "Right here!"

Roscoe knew his princess had finally returned his letter even before he saw her name. He retreated to his cell and asked his cellmate to step out for a second just in case he got emotional. The only acceptable emotion in prison is anger so anything else had to be done in private.

"No problem, old school," his new cellmate replied and hopped off his bunk. The prison had a system of placing younger inmates with vets hoping they could school them on how to survive. There's rules to this prison shit and violating them will get you killed.

"Let's see here..." Roscoe said and opened the taped enveloped once more. It had already been opened once to check for contraband before passed out. A small picture fell out and he knew he was a grandfather again. He could see his daughter's face in the child's and knew his baby girl was now a mother. He pulled out the letter and read...

*'Sup dad. Daddy, pops, shit, I'on know what to call you. Anyway, I'm sorry I didn't write back sooner. It's rough out here in these streets. Especially without a father. I guess that's what I'll call you, father.*

*As you see, I had a baby. His name is Roscoe. His father is dead so I got him. I got a new boyfriend named Seven and Roscoe is good. Me and Unique moved down south. We in school and doing good.*

*I just wanted to let you know what happened to Reef. Our block was beefing with them niggas from170th. A young dude named Kidd is the*

*one who killed him. Kidd Johnson, he there with you. He killed my broth-*
*er. What you gone do?*

*Peace, Reign*

"I'm gone kill the nigga! What you think? I'm Roscoe Raheem from High Bridge!" he announced, getting piped up. He knew exactly who Kidd was and where he could be found. He stuck his head out and called his cellmate. "Yo, B. I'm done. Come let me talk to you about something."

"Sure. Sup, old school?" Kidd asked when he came back into the cell.

"Got a message from my daughter, Reign. She told me all about you," Roscoe said, putting the privacy sheet over the window.

"Word!" Kidd said and smiled at the baby picture on the bed.

"Word. Told me you killed my son, Reef," he said and wrapped his meaty arm around his scrawny neck.

Kidd clawed at the big beefy arms and struggled to get free but it was not to be. He felt his feet leave the floor and his life leaving his body. He looked at the baby picture on the man's bed as his soul was literally squeezed from his body.

Roscoe fixed him up with his own sheet around his neck. He eased out the cell so he could finish working out and discover the suicide when he returned.

Life is funny like that. Chilling one minute and dead the next.